GHOST STORIES

A

GHOST STORIES

BY

E. AND H. HERON

LONDON
C. ARTHUR PEARSON, LIMITED
HENRIETTA STREET, W.C.
1917

SECOND IMPRESSION.

CONTENTS

INTRODUCTION

HAVE ghosts any existence outside our own fancy and emotion ? This is the question with which the new century concerns itself more and more, for, though a vast amount of evidence with regard to occult phenomena already exists, the ultimate answer has yet to be supplied. In this connection it may not generally be known that, as one of the first steps towards reducing Psychology to the lines of an exact science, an attempt has been made to classify spirits and ghosts, with the result that some very bizarre and terrible theories have been put forward—things undreamt of outside the circle of the select few.

With a view to meeting the widespread interest in these matters, the following series of ghost stories is laid before the public. They have been gathered out of a large number of supernatural experiences with which Mr. Flaxman Low—under the thin disguise of which name many are sure to recognise one of the leading scientists of the day, with whose works on Psychology and kindred subjects they are familiar—has been more or less connected. He is, moreover, the first student in this field of inquiry who has had the boldness and originality to break free from old and conventional methods, and to approach the elucidation of so-called supernatural problems on the lines of natural law.

The details of these stories have been supplied by the narratives of those most concerned, supplemented by the clear and ample notes which Mr. Flaxman Low has had the courtesy to place in our hands.

For obvious reasons, the *exact* localities where these events are said to have happened are in every case merely indicated.

THE STORY OF THE SPANIARDS,

HAMMERSMITH

LIEUTENANT RODERICK HOUSTON, of H.M.S. *Sphinx*, had practically nothing beyond his pay, and he was beginning to be very tired of the West African station, when he received the pleasant intelligence that a relative had left him a legacy. This consisted of a satisfactory sum in ready money and a house in Hammersmith, which was rated at over £200 a year, and was said in addition to be comfortably furnished. Houston, therefore, counted on its rental to bring his income up to a fairly desirable figure. Further information from home, however, showed him that he had been rather premature in his expectations, whereupon, being a man of action, he applied for two months' leave, and came home to look after his affairs himself.

When he had been a week in London he arrived at the conclusion that he could not possibly hope single-handed to tackle the difficulties which presented themselves. He accordingly wrote the following letter to his friend, Flaxman Low :

The Spaniards, Hammersmith, 23-3-1892.

DEAR LOW,—Since we parted some three years ago, I have heard very little of you. It was only yesterday that I met our mutual friend, Sammy Smith (" Silkworm " of our schooldays), who told me that your studies have developed in a new direction, and that you are now a good deal interested in psychical subjects. If this be so, I hope to induce you to come and stay with me here for a few days by promising to introduce you to a problem in your own line. I am just now living at " The Spaniards," a house that has lately been left to me, and which in the first instance was built by an old fellow named Van Nuysen, who married a great-aunt of mine. It is a good house, but there is said to be " something wrong," with it. It lets easily, but unluckily the tenants cannot be persuaded to remain above a week or two. They complain that the place is haunted by something—presumably a ghost—because its vagaries bear just that brand of inconsequence which stamps the common run of manifestations.

It occurs to me that you may care to investigate the matter with me. If so, send me a wire when to expect you.

Yours ever,

RODERICK HOUSTON.

Houston waited in some anxiety for an answer. Low was the sort of man one could rely on in almost any emergency. Sammy Smith had told him a characteristic anecdote of Low's career at Oxford, where, although his intellectual triumphs may be forgotten, he will always be remembered by the story that when Sands, of Queen's, fell ill on the day before the 'Varsity sports, a telegram was sent to Low's rooms : " Sands ill. You must do the hammer for us." Low's reply was pithy : " I'll be there." Thereupon he finished the treatise upon which he was engaged, and next day his strong, lean figure was to be seen swinging the hammer amidst vociferous cheering, for that was the occasion on which he not only won the event, but beat the record.

On the fifth day Low's answer came from Vienna. As he read it, Houston recalled the high forehead, long neck—with its accompanying low collar—and thin moustache of his scholarly, athletic friend, and smiled. There was so much more in Flaxman Low than anyone gave him credit for.

MY DEAR HOUSTON,—Very glad to hear of you again. In response to your kind invitation, I thank you for the opportunity of meeting the ghost, and still more for the pleasure of your companionship.   I came here to inquire into a somewhat similar affair. I hope, however, to be able to leave to-morrow, and will be with you sometime on Friday evening.

Very sincerely yours,

FLAXMAN LOW.

P.S.—By the way, will it be convenient to give your servants a holiday during the term of my visit, as, if my investigations are to be of any value, not a grain of dust must be disturbed in your house, excepting by ourselves ?—F. L.

"The Spaniards" was within some fifteen minutes' walk of Hammersmith Bridge. Set in the midst of a fairly respectable neighbourhood, it presented an odd contrast to the commonplace dullness of the narrow streets crowded about it. As Flaxman Low drove up in the evening light, he reflected that the house might have come from the back of beyond—it gave an impression of something old-world and something exotic.

It was surrounded by a ten-foot wall, above which the upper storey was visible, and Low decided that this intensely English house still gave some curious suggestion of the tropics. The interior of the house carried out the same idea, with its sense of space and air, cool tints and wide, matted passages.

"So you have seen something yourself since you came?" Low said, as they sat at dinner, for Houston had arranged that meals should be sent in for them from an hotel.

"I've heard tapping up and down the passage upstairs. It is an uncarpeted landing which runs the whole length of the house. One night, when I was quicker than usual, I saw what looked like a bladder disappear into one of the bedrooms—your room it is to be, by the way—and the door closed behind it," replied Houston discontentedly. "The usual meaningless antics of a ghost."

"What had the tenants who lived here to say about it?" went on Low.

"Most of the people saw and heard just what I have told you, and promptly went away. The only one who stood out for a little while was old Filderg—you know the man? Twenty years

ago he made an effort to cross the Australian
deserts—he stopped for eight weeks. When he
left he saw the house-agent, and said he was
afraid he had done a little shooting practice in
the upper passage, and he hoped it wouldn't
count against him in the bill, as it was done in
defence of his life. He said something had
jumped on to the bed and tried to strangle him.
He described it as cold and glutinous, and he
pursued it down the passage, firing at it. He
advised the owner to have the house pulled down ;
but, of course, my cousin did nothing of the kind.
It's a very good house, and he did not see the sense
of spoiling his property."

"That's very true," replied Flaxman Low,
looking round. "Mr. Van Nuysen had been
in the West Indies, and kept his liking for spacious
rooms."

"Where did you hear anything about him ? "
asked Houston in surprise.

"I have heard nothing beyond what you
told me in your letter ; but I see a couple of
bottles of Gulf weed and a lace-plant ornament,
such as people used to bring from the West Indies
in former days."

"Perhaps I should tell you the history of the
old man," said Houston doubtfully ; "but we
aren't proud of it ! "

Flaxman Low considered a moment.

"When was the ghost seen for the first time ? "

"When the first tenant took the house. It
was let after old Van Nuysen's time."

"Then it may clear the way if you will tell
me something of him."

"He owned sugar plantations in Trinidad,
where he passed the greater part of his life,

while his wife mostly remained in England—
incompatibility of temper it was said. When he
came home for good and built this house they
still lived apart, my aunt declaring that nothing
on earth would persuade her to return to him.
In course of time he became a confirmed invalid,
and he then insisted on my aunt joining him.
She lived here for perhaps a year, when she
was found dead in bed one morning—in your
room."

"What caused her death ? "

"She had been in the habit of taking narcotics,
and it was supposed that she smothered herself
while under their influence."

"That doesn't sound very satisfactory," remarked Flaxman Low.

"Her husband was satisfied with it anyhow,
and it was no one else's business. The family
were only too glad to have the affair hushed
up."

"And what became of Mr. Van Nuysen ? "

"That I can't tell you. He disappeared a
short time after. Search was made for him in
the usual way, but nobody knows to this day
what became of him."

"Ah, that was strange, as he was such an
invalid," said Low, and straightway fell into a
long fit of abstraction, from which he was roused
by hearing Houston curse the incurable foolishness
and imbecility of ghostly behaviour. Flaxman
woke up at this. He broke a walnut thoughtfully
and began in a gentle voice :

"My dear fellow, we are apt to be hasty in
our condemnation of the general behaviour of
ghosts. It may appear incalculably foolish in
our eyes, and I admit there often seems to be a

total absence of any apparent object or intelligent action. But remember that what appears to us to be foolishness may be wisdom in the spirit world, since our unready senses can only catch broken glimpses of what is, I have not the slightest doubt, a coherent whole, if we could trace the connection."

"There may be something in that," replied Houston indifferently. "People naturally say that this ghost is the ghost of old Van Nuysen. But what connection can possibly exist between what I have told you of him and the manifestations—a tapping up and down the passage and the drawing about of a bladder like a child at play ? It sounds idiotic ! "

" Certainly. Yet it need not necessarily be so. There are isolated facts, we must look for the links which lie between. Suppose a saddle and a horse-shoe were to be shown to a man who had never seen a horse, I doubt whether he, however intelligent, could evolve the connecting idea ! The ways of spirits are strange to us simply because we need further data to help us to interpret them."

" It's a new point of view," returned Houston, " but upon my word, you know, Low, I think you're wasting your time ! "

Flaxman Low smiled slowly ; his grave, melancholy face brightened.

" I have," said he, " gone somewhat deeply into the subject. In other sciences one reasons by analogy. Psychology is unfortunately a science with a future but without a past, or more probably it is a lost science of the ancients. However that may be, we stand to-day on the frontier of an unknown world, and progress

is the result of individual effort ; each solution
of difficult phenomena forms a step towards the
solution of the next problem. In this case,
for example, the bladder-like object may be the
key to the mystery."

Houston yawned.

" It all seems pretty senseless, but perhaps
you may be able to read reason into it. If it
were anything tangible, anything a man could
meet with his fists, it would be easier."

" I entirely agree with you. But suppose we
deal with this affair as it stands, on similar lines,
I mean on prosaic, rational lines, as we should
deal with a purely human mystery."

" My dear fellow," returned Houston, pushing
his chair back from the table wearily, " you
shall do just as you like, only get rid of the
ghost ! "

For some time after Low's arrival nothing very
special happened. The tappings continued, and
more than once Low had been in time to see
the bladder disappear into the closing door of
his bedroom, though, unluckily, he never chanced
to be inside the room on these occasions, and
however quickly he followed the bladder, he
never succeeded in seeing anything further.
He made a thorough examination of the house,
and left no space unaccounted for in his careful
measurement. There were no cellars, and the
foundation of the house consisted of a thick
layer of concrete.

At length, on the sixth night, an event took
place, which, as Flaxman Low remarked, came
very near to putting an end to the investigations
as far as he was concerned. For the preceding
two nights he and Houston had kept watch

in the hope of getting a glimpse of the person
or thing which tapped so persistently up and down
the passage. But they were disappointed, for
there were no manifestations. On the third
evening, therefore, Low went off to his room a
little earlier than usual, and fell asleep almost
immediately.

He says he was awakened by feeling a heavy
weight upon his feet, something that seemed
inert and motionless. He recollected that he
had left the gas burning, but the room was now
in darkness.

Next he was aware that the thing on the bed
had slowly shifted, and was gradually travelling
up towards his chest. How it came on the bed
he had no idea. Had it leaped or climbed ?
The sensation he experienced as it moved was
of some ponderous, pulpy body, not crawling
or creeping, but spreading ! It was horrible !
He tried to move his lower limbs, but could
not because of the deadening weight. A feeling
of drowsiness began to overpower him, and a
deadly cold, such as he said he had before felt
at sea when in the neighbourhood of icebergs,
chilled upon the air.

With a violent struggle he managed to free
his arms, but the thing grew more irresistible as
it spread upwards. Then he became conscious
of a pair of glassy eyes, with livid, everted lids,
looking into his own. Whether they were human
eyes or beast eyes, he could not tell, but they
were watery, like the eyes of a dead fish, and
gleamed with a pale, internal lustre.

Then he owns he grew afraid. But he was
still cool enough to notice one peculiarity about
this ghastly visitant—although the head was

B

within a few inches of his own, he could detect
no breathing. It dawned upon him that he was
about to be suffocated, for, by the same method
of extension, the thing was now coming over his
face ! It felt cold and clammy, like a mass of
mucilage or a monstrous snail. And every instant
the weight became greater. He is a powerful
man, and he struck with his fists again and again
at the head. Some substance yielded under
the blows with a sickening sensation of bruised
flesh.

With a lucky twist he raised himself in the bed
and battered away with all the force he was
capable of in his cramped position. The only
effect was an occasional shudder or quake that
ran through the mass as his half-arm blows rained
upon it. At last, by chance, his hand knocked
against the candle beside him. In a moment
he recollected the matches. He seized the box,
and struck a light.

As he did so, the lump slid to the floor. He
sprang out of bed, and lit the candle. He felt
a cold touch upon his leg, but when he looked
down there was nothing to be seen. The door,
which he had locked overnight, was now open,
and he rushed out into the passage. All was
still and silent with the throbbing vacancy of
night time.

After searching round, he returned to his room.
The bed still gave ample proof of the struggle
that had taken place, and by his watch he saw
the hour to be between two and three.

As there seemed nothing more to be done, he
put on his dressing-gown, lit his pipe, and sat
down to write an account of the experience he
had **just** passed through for the Psychical

Research Society—from which paper the above is an abstract.

He is a man of strong nerves, but he could not disguise from himself that he had been at hand-grips with some grotesque form of death. What might be the nature of his assailant he could not determine, but his experience was supported by the attack which had been made on Filderg, and also—it was impossible to avoid the conclusion—by the manner of Mrs. Van Nuysen's death.

He thought the whole situation over carefully in connection with the tapping and the disappearing bladder, but, turn these events how he would, he could make nothing of them. They were entirely incongruous. A little later he went and made a shakedown in Houston's room.

"What was the thing?" asked Houston, when Low had ended his story of the encounter.

Low shrugged his shoulders.

"At least it proves that Filderg did not dream," he said.

"But this is monstrous! We are more in the dark than ever. There's nothing for it but to have the house pulled down. Let us leave to-day."

"Don't be in a hurry, my dear fellow. You would rob me of a very great pleasure; besides, we may be on the verge of some valuable discovery. This series of manifestations is even more interesting than the Vienna mystery I was telling you of."

"Discovery or not," replied the other, "I don't like it."

The first thing next morning Low went out for a quarter of an hour. Before breakfast a man with a barrowful of sand came into the garden. Low looked up from his paper, leant out of the window, and gave some order.

When Houston came down a few minutes later he saw the yellowish heap on the lawn with some surprise.

" Hullo ! What's this ? " he asked.

" I ordered it," replied Low.

" All right. What's it for ? "

" To help us in our investigations. Our visitor is capable of being felt, and he or it left a very distinct impression on the bed. Hence I gather it can also leave an impression on sand. It would be an immense advance if we could arrive at any correct notion of what sort of feet the ghost walks on. I propose to spread a layer of this sand in the upper passage, and the result should be footmarks if the tapping comes to-night."

That evening the two men made a fire in Houston's bedroom, and sat there smoking and talking, to leave the ghost " a free run for once," as Houston phrased it. The tapping was heard at the usual hour, and presently the accustomed pause at the other end of the passage and the quiet closing of the door.

Low heaved a long sigh of satisfaction as he listened.

" That's my bedroom door," he said ; " I know the sound of it perfectly. In the morning, and with the help of daylight, we shall see what we shall see."

As soon as there was light enough for the purpose of examining the footprints, Low roused Houston.

Houston was as full of excitement as a boy,

but his spirits fell by the time he had passed from end to end of the passage.

"There are marks," he said, "but they are as perplexing as everything else about this haunting brute, whatever it is. I suppose you think this is the print left by the thing which attacked you the night before last?"

"I fancy it is," said Low, who was still bending over the floor eagerly. "What do you make of it, Houston?"

"The brute has only one leg, to start with," replied Houston, "and that leaves the mark of a large, clawless pad! It's some animal— some ghoulish monster!"

"On the contrary," said Low, "I think we have now every reason to conclude that it is a man?"

"A man? What man ever left footmarks like these?"

"Look at these hollows and streaks at the sides; they are the traces of the sticks we have heard tapping."

"You don't convince me," returned Houston doggedly.

"Let us wait another twenty-four hours, and to-morrow night, if nothing further occurs, I will give you my conclusions. Think it over. The tapping, the bladder, and the fact that Mr. Van Nuysen had lived in Trinidad. Add to these things this single pad-like print. Does nothing strike you by way of a solution?"

Houston shook his head.

"Nothing. And I fail to connect any of these things with what happened both to you and Filderg."

"Ah! now," said Flaxman Low, his face

clouding a little, " I confess you lead me into a somewhat different region, though to me the connection is perfect."

Houston raised his eyebrows and laughed.

" If you can unravel this tangle of hints and events and diagnose the ghost, I shall be extremely astonished," he said. " What can you make of the footless impression ? "

" Something, I hope. In fact, that mark may be a clue—an outrageous one, perhaps, but still a clue."

That evening the weather broke, and by night the storm had risen to a gale, accompanied by sharp bursts of rain.

" It's a noisy night," remarked Houston ; " I don't suppose we'll hear the ghost, supposing it does turn up."

This was after dinner, as they were about to go into the smoking-room. Houston, finding the gas low in the hall, stopped to turn it higher ; at the same time asking Low to see if the jet on the upper landing was also alight.

Flaxman Low glanced up and uttered a slight exclamation, which brought Houston to his side.

Looking down at them from over the banisters was a face—a blotched, yellowish face, flanked by two swollen, protruding ears, the whole aspect being strangely leonine. It was but a glimpse, a clash of meeting glances, as it were, a glare of defiance, and the face was quickly withdrawn as the two men literally leapt up the stairs.

" There's nothing here," exclaimed Houston, after a search had been carried out through every room above.

"I didn't suppose we'd find anything," returned Low.

"This fairly knots up the thread," said Houston. "You can't pretend to unravel it now."

"Come down," said Low briefly ; " I'm ready to give you my opinion, such as it is."

Once in the smoking-room, Houston busied himself in turning on all the light he could procure, then he saw to securing the windows, and piled up an immense fire, while Flaxman Low, who, as usual, had a cigarette in his mouth, sat on the edge of the table and watched him with some amusement.

"You saw that abominable face ? " cried Houston, as he threw himself into a chair. " It was as material as yours or mine. But where did he go to ? He must be somewhere about."

"We saw him clearly. That is sufficient for our purpose."

"You are very good at enumerating points, Low. Now just listen to my list. The difficulties grow with every fresh discovery. We're at a deadlock now, I take it ? The sticks and the tapping point to an old man, the playing with a bladder to a child ; the footmark might be the pad of a tiger minus claws, yet the thing that attacked you at night was cold and pulpy. And, lastly, by way of a wind-up, we see a lion-like, human face ! If you can make all these items square with each other, I'll be happy to hear what you have got to say."

"You must first allow me to ask you a question. I understood you to say that no blood relationship existed between you and old Mr. Van Nuysen ? "

" Certainly not. He was quite an outsider,"
answered Houston brusquely.

" In that case you are welcome to my conclusions. All the things you have mentioned
point to one explanation. This house is haunted
by the ghost of Mr. Van Nuysen, and he was
a leper."

Houston stood up and stared at his companion.

" What a horrible notion ! I must say I
fail to see how you have arrived at such a conclusion."

" Take the chain of evidence in rather different
order," said Low. " Why should a man tap
with a stick ? "

" Generally because he's blind."

" In cases of blindness, one stick is used for
guidance. Here we have two for support."

" A man who has lost the use of his feet."

" Exactly ; a man who has from some cause
partially lost the use of his feet."

" But the bladder and the lion-like face ? "
went on Houston.

" The bladder, or what seemed to us to resemble
a bladder, was one of his feet, contorted by the
disease and probably swathed in linen, which
foot he dragged rather than used ; consequently,
in passing through a door, for example, he would
be in the habit of drawing it in after him. Now,
as regards the single footmark we saw. In one
form of leprosy, the smaller bones of the
extremities frequently fall away. The pad-like
impression was, as I believe, the mark of the
other foot—a toeless foot which he used, because
in a more advanced stage of the disease the
maimed hand or foot heals and becomes
callous."

"Go on," said Houston; "it sounds as if it might be true. And the lion-like face I can account for myself. I have been in China, and have seen it before in lepers."

"Mr. Van Nuysen had been in Trinidad for many years, as we know, and while there he probably contracted the disease."

"I suppose so. After his return," added Houston, "he shut himself up almost entirely, and gave out that he was a martyr to rheumatic gout, this awful thing being the true explanation."

"It also accounts for Mrs. Van Nuysen's determination not to return to her husband."

Houston appeared much disturbed.

"We can't drop it here, Low," he said, in a constrained voice. "There is a good deal more to be cleared up yet. Can you tell me more?"

"From this point I find myself on less certain ground," replied Low unwillingly. "I merely offer a suggestion, remember—I don't ask you to accept it. I believe Mrs. Van Nuysen was murdered!"

"What?" exclaimed Houston. "By her husband?"

"Indications tend that way."

"But, my good fellow——"

"He suffocated her and then made away with himself. It is a pity that his body was not recovered. The condition of the remains would be the only really satisfactory test of my theory. If the skeleton could even now be found, the fact that he was a leper would be finally settled."

There was a prolonged pause until Houston put another question.

"Wait a minute, Low," he said. "Ghosts are

admittedly immaterial.   In this instance our
spook has an extremely palpable body.   Surely
this is rather unusual ?   You have made everything else more or less plain.   Can you tell
me why this dead leper should have tried to
murder you and old Filderg ?   And also how he
came to have the actual physical power to do
so ? "

Low removed his cigarette to look thoughtfully at the end of it.   " Now I lapse into the
purely theoretical," he answered.   " Cases have
been known where the assumption of diabolical
agency is apparently justifiable."

" Diabolical agency ?—I don't follow you."

" I will try to make myself clear, though the
subject is still in a stage of vagueness and
immaturity.   Van Nuysen committed a murder
of exceptional atrocity, and afterwards killed
himself.   Now, bodies of suicides are known
to be peculiarly susceptible to spiritual influences,
even to the point of arrested corruption.   Add to
this our knowledge that the highest aim of an
evil spirit is to gain possession of a material body.
If I carried out my theory to its logical conclusion, I should say that Van Nuysen's body
is hidden somewhere on these premises—that
this body is intermittently animated by some
spirit, which at certain periods is forced to re-
enact the gruesome tragedy of the Van Nuysens.
Should any living person chance to occupy the
position of the first victim, so much the worse for
him ! "

For some minutes Houston made no remark
on this singular expression of opinion.

" But have you ever met with anything of the
sort before ? " he said at last.

"I can recall," replied Flaxman Low thoughtfully, " quite a number of cases which would seem
to bear out this hypothesis. Among them a
curious problem of haunting exhaustively
examined by Busner in the early part of 1888,
at which I was myself lucky enough to assist.
Indeed, I may add that the affair which I have
recently been engaged upon in Vienna offers
some rather similar features. There, however,
we had to stop short of excavation, by which
alone any specific results might have been
attained."

"Then you are of opinion," said Houston,
"that pulling the house to pieces might cast
some further light upon this affair ? "

"I cannot see any better course," said Mr.
Low.

Then Houston closed the discussion by a very
definite declaration.

"This house shall come down ! "

So "The Spaniards" was pulled down.

Such is the story of " The Spaniards," Hammersmith, and it has been given the first place in this
series because, although it may not be of so
strange a nature as some that will follow it, yet
it seems to us to embody in a high degree the
peculiar methods by which Mr. Flaxman Low
is wont to approach these cases.

The work of demolition, begun at the earliest
possible moment, did not occupy very long,
and during its early stages, under the boarding
at an angle of the landing was found a skeleton.
Several of the phalanges were missing, and other
indications also established beyond a doubt the
fact that the remains were the remains of a
leper.

The skeleton is now in the museum of one of
our city hospitals. It bears a scientific ticket,
and is the only evidence extant of the correctness
of Mr. Flaxman Low's methods and the possible
truth of his extraordinary theories.

II

THE STORY OF MEDHANS LEA

THE following story has been put together from the account of the affair given by Nare-Jones, sometime house-surgeon at Bart's, of his strange terror and experiences both in Medhans Lea and the pallid avenue between the beeches ; of the narrative of Savelsan, of what he saw and heard in the billiard room and afterwards ; of the silent and indisputable witness of big, bullnecked Harland himself ; and, lastly, of the conversation which subsequently took place between these three men and Mr. Flaxman Low, the noted psychologist.

It was by the merest chance that Harland and his two guests spent that memorable evening of the 18th of January, 1899, in the house of Medhans Lea. The house stands on the slope of a partially-wooded ridge in one of the Midland Counties. It faces south, and overlooks a wide valley bounded by the blue outlines of the Bredon hills. The place is secluded, the nearest dwelling being a small public-house at the cross roads some mile and a half from the lodge gates.

Medhans Lea is famous for its long straight

avenue of beeches, and for other things. Harland, when he signed the lease, was thinking of the avenue of beeches ; not of the other things, of which he knew nothing until later.

Harland had made his money by running tea plantations in Assam, and he owned all the virtues and faults of a man who has spent most of his life abroad. The first time he visited the house he weighed seventeen stone and ended most of his sentences with " don't yer know ? " His ideas could hardly be said to travel on the higher planes of thought, and his chief aim in life was to keep himself down to the seventeen stone. He had a red neck and a blue eye, and was a muscular, inoffensive, good-natured man, with courage to spare, and an excellent voice for accompanying the banjo.

After signing the lease, he found that Medhans Lea needed an immense amount of putting in order and decorating. While this was being done, he came backwards and forwards to the nearest provincial town, where he stopped at a hotel, driving out almost daily to superintend the arrangements of his new habitation. Thus he had been away for the Christmas and New Year, but about the 15th January he returned to the Red Lion, accompanied by his friends Nare-Jones and Savelsan, who proposed to move with him into his new house during the course of the ensuing week.

The immediate cause of their visit to Medhans Lea on the evening of the 18th inst. was the fact that the billiard table at the Red Lion was not fit, as Harland remarked, to play shinty on, while there was an excellent table just put in at Medhans Lea, where the big billiard-room in the

left wing had a wide window with a view down a
portion of the beech avenue.

"Hang it!" said Harland, "I wish they
would hurry up with the house. The painters
aren't out of it yet, and the people don't come
to the Lodge till Monday."

"It's a pity, too," remarked Savelsan regret-
fully, "when you think of that table."

Savelsan was an enthusiast in billiards, who
spent all the time he could spare from his business,
which happened to be teabroking, at the game.
He was the more sorry for the delay, since Harland
was one of the few men he knew to whom it was
not necessary to give points.

"It's a ripping table," returned Harland.
"Tell you what," he added, struck by a happy
idea, "I'll send out Thoms to make things
straight for us to-morrow, and we'll put a case
of syphons and a bottle of whisky under the seat
of the trap, and drive over for a game after dinner."

The other two agreed to this arrangement,
but in the morning Nare-Jones found himself
obliged to run up to London to see about
securing a berth as ship's doctor. It was settled,
however, that on his return he was to follow
Harland and Savelsan to Medhans Lea.

He got back by the 8.30, entirely delighted,
because he had booked a steamer bound for the
Persian Gulf and Karachi, and had gained the
cheering intelligence that a virulent type of
cholera was lying in wait for the advent of the
Mecca pilgrims in at any rate two of the chief
ports of call, which would give him precisely the
experience he desired.

Having dined, and the night being fine, he
ordered a dogcart to take him out to Medhans

Lea. The moon had just risen by the time he reached the entrance to the avenue, and as he was beginning to feel cold he pulled up, intending to walk to the house. Then he dismissed the boy and cart, a carriage having been ordered to come for the whole party after midnight. Narc-Jones stopped to light a cigar before entering the avenue, then he walked past the empty lodge. He moved briskly in the best possible temper with himself and all the world. The night was still, and his collar up, his feet fell silently on the dry carriage road, while his mind was away on blue water forecasting his voyage on the s.s. *Sumatra*.

He says he was quite halfway up the avenue before he became conscious of anything unusual. Looking up at the sky, he noticed what a bright, clear night it was, and how sharply defined the outline of the beeches stood out against the vault of heaven. The moon was yet low, and threw netted shadows of bare twigs and branches on the road which ran between black lines of trees in an almost straight vista up to the dead grey face of the house now barely two hundred yards away. Altogether it struck him as forming a pallid picture, etched in like a steel engraving in black, and grey, and white.

He was thinking of this when he was aware of words spoken rapidly in his ear, and he turned half expecting to see someone behind him. No one was visible. He had not caught the words, nor could he define the voice ; but a vague conviction of some horrible meaning fixed itself in his consciousness.

The night was very still, ahead of him the house glimmered grey and shuttered in the moonlight.

He shook himself, and walked on oppressed by
a novel sensation compounded of disgust and
childish fear ; and still, from behind his shoulder,
came the evil, voiceless murmuring.

He admits that he passed the end of the avenue
at an amble, and was abreast of a semi-circle
of shrubbery, when a small object was thrust
out from the shadow of the bushes, and lay in
the open light. Though the night was peculiarly
still, it fluttered and balanced a moment, as if
windblown, then came in skimming flights to
his feet. He picked it up and made for the door,
which yielded to his hand, and he flung it to and
bolted it behind him.

Once in the warmly-lit hall his senses returned,
and he waited to recover breath and composure
before facing the two men whose voices and
laughter came from a room on his right. But
the door of the room was thrown open, and the
burly figure of Harland in his shirt sleeves
appeared on the threshold.

" Hullo, Jones, that you ? Come along ! "
he said genially.

" Bless me ! " exclaimed Nare-Jones irritably,
" there's not a light in any of the windows. It
might be a house of the dead ! "

Harland stared at him, but all he said was :
" Have a whisky-and-soda ? "

Savelsan, who was leaning over the billiard
table, trying side-strokes with his back to Nare-
Jones, added :

" Did you expect us to illuminate the place
for you ? There's not a soul in the house but
ourselves."

" Say when," said Harland, poising the bottle
over a glass.

c

Nare-Jones laid down what he held in his hand on the corner of the billiard table, and took up his glass.

"What in creation's this ? " asked Savelsan.

"I don't know ; the wind blew it to my feet just outside," replied Nare-Jones, between two long pulls at the whisky-and-soda.

"*Blown* to your feet ? " repeated Savelsan, taking up the thing and weighing it in his hand. "It must be blowing a hurricane then."

"It isn't blowing at all," returned Nare-Jones blankly. "The night is dead calm."

For the object that had fluttered and rolled so lightly across the turf and gravel was a small battered, metal calf, made of some heavy brass amalgam.

Savelsan looked incredulously into Nare-Jones' face, and laughed.

"What's wrong with you ? You look queer."

Nare-Jones laughed too ; he was already ashamed of the last ten minutes.

Harland was meantime examining the metal calf.

"It's a Bengali idol," he said, "It's been knocked about a good bit, by Jove ! You say it blew out of the shrubbery ? "

"Like a bit of paper, I give you my word, though there was not a breath of wind going," admitted Nare-Jones.

"Seems odd, don't yer know ? " remarked Harland carelessly. "Now you two fellows had better begin ; I'll mark."

Nare-Jones happened to be in form that night, and Savelsan became absorbed in the delightful difficulty of giving him a sound thrashing.

Suddenly Savelsan paused in his stroke.

" What the sin's that ? " he asked.

They stood listening. A thin, broken crying could be heard.

" Sounds like green plover," remarked Nare-Jones, chalking his cue.

" It's a kitten they've shut up somewhere," said Harland.

" That's a child, and in the deuce of a fright, too," said Savelsan. " You'd better go and tuck it up in its little bed, Harland," he added, with a laugh.

Harland opened the door. There could no longer be any doubt about the sounds ; the stifled shrieks and thin whimpering told of a child in the extremity of pain or fear.

" It's upstairs," said Harland. " I'm going to see."

Nare-Jones picked up a lamp and followed him.

" I stay here," said Savelsan sitting down by the fire.

In the hall the two men stopped and listened again. It is hard to locate a noise, but this seemed to come from the upper landing.

" Poor little beggar ! " exclaimed Harland, as he bounded up the staircase. The bedroom doors opening on the square central landing above were all locked, the keys being on the outside. But the crying led them into a side passage which ended in a single room.

" It's in here, and the door's locked," said Nare-Jones. " Call out and see who's there."

But Harland was set on business. He flung his weight against the panel, and the door burst open, the lock ricochetting noisily into a corner. As they passed in, the crying ceased abruptly.

Harland stood in the centre of the room, while Nare-Jones held up the light to look round.

"The dickens!" exclaimed Harland exhaustively.

The room was entirely empty.

Not so much as a cupboard broke the smooth surface of the walls, only the two low windows and the door by which they had entered.

"This is the room above the billiard-room, isn't it?" said Nare-Jones at last.

"Yes. This is the only one I have not had furnished yet. I thought I might——"

He stopped short, for behind them burst out a peal of harsh, mocking laughter, that rang and echoed between the bare walls.

Both men swung round simultaneously, and both caught a glimpse of a tall, thin figure in black, rocking with laughter in the doorway, but when they turned it was gone. They dashed out into the passage and landing. No one was to be seen. The doors were locked as before, and the staircase and hall were vacant.

After making a prolonged search through every corner of the house, they went back to Savelsan in the billiard-room.

"What were you laughing about? What is it anyway?" began Savelsan at once.

"It's nothing. And we didn't laugh," replied Nare-Jones definitely.

"But I heard you," insisted Savelsan. "And where's the child?"

"I wish you'd go up and find it," returned Harland grimly, "We heard the laughing and saw, or thought we saw, a man in black——"

"Something like a priest in a cassock," put in Nare-Jones,

"Yes, like a priest," assented Harland, "but as we turned he disappeared."

Savelsan sat down and gazed from one to the other of his companions.

"The house behaves as if it was haunted," he remarked ; "only there is no such thing as an authenticated ghost outside the experiences of the Psychical Research Society. I'd ask the Society down if I were you, Harland. You never can tell what you may find in these old houses."

"It's not an old house," replied Harland. "It was built somewhere about '40. I certainly saw that man ; and, look to it, Savelsan, I'll find out who or what he is. That I swear ! The English law makes no allowance for ghosts— nor will I."

"You'll have your hands full, or I'm mistaken," exclaimed Savelsan, grinning. "A ghost that laughs and cries in a breath, and rolls battered idols about your front door, is not to be trifled with. The night is young yet—not much past eleven. I vote for a peg all round and then I'll finish off Jones."

Harland, sunk in a fit of sullen abstraction, sat on a settee, and watched them. On a sudden he said :

"It's turned beastly cold."

"There's a beastly smell, you mean," corrected Savelsan crossly, as he went round the table. He had made a break of forty and did not want to be interrupted. "The draught is from the window."

"I've not noticed it before this evening," said Harland, as he opened the shutters to make sure.

As he did so the night air rushed in heavy

with the smell as of an old well that has not been
uncovered for years, a smell of slime and un-
wholesome wetness. The lower part of the
window was wide open and Harland banged it
down.

"It's abominable!" he said, with an angry
sniff. "Enough to give us all typhoid."

"Only dead leaves," remarked Nare-Jones.
"There are the rotten leaves of twenty winters
under the trees and outside this window. I
noticed them when we came over on Tuesday."

"I'll have them cleared away to-morrow. I
wonder how Thoms came to leave this window
open," grumbled Harland, as he closed and
bolted the shutter. "What do you say—
forty-five?" and he went over to mark it up.

The game went on for some time, and Nare-
Jones was lying across the table with the cue
poised, when he heard a slight sound behind him.
Looking round he saw Harland, his face flushed
and angry, passing softly—wonderfully softly
for so big a man, Nare-Jones remembers thinking—along the angle of the wall towards the
window.

All three men unite in declaring that they were
watching the shutter, which opened inwards as
if thrust by some furtive hand from outside.
At the moment Nare-Jones and Savelsan were
standing directly opposite to it on the further
side of the table, while Harland crouched behind
the shutter intent on giving the intruder a lesson.

As the shutter unfolded to its utmost the two
men opposite saw a face pressed against the glass,
a furrowed evil face, with a wide laugh perched
upon its sinister features.

There was a second of absolute stillness, and

Narc-Jones' eyes met those other eyes with the
fascinated horror of a mutual understanding, as
all the foul fancies that had pursued him in the
avenue poured back into his mind.

With an uncontrollable impulse of resentment,
he snatched a billiard ball from the table and flung
it with all his strength at the face. The ball
crashed through the glass and through the face
beyond it! The glass fell shattered, but the
face remained for an instant peering and grinning
at the aperture, then as Harland sprang forward
it was gone.

" The ball went clean through it ! " said Savelsan with a gasp.

They crowded to the window, and throwing
up the sash, leant out. The dank smell clung
about the air, a boat-shaped moon glimmered
between the bare branches, and on the white
drive beyond the shrubbery the billiard ball
could be seen a shining spot under the moon.
Nothing more.

" What was it ? " asked Harland.

" ' Only a face at the window,' " quoted
Savelsan with an awkward attempt at making
light of his own scare. " Devilish queer face too,
eh, Jones ? "

" I wish I'd got him ! " returned Harland
frowning. " I'm not going to put up with any
tricks about the place, don't yer know ? "

" You'd bottle any tramp loafing round,"
said Narc-Jones.

Harland looked down at his immense arms
outlined in his shirt-sleeves.

" I could that," he answered. " But this
chap—did you hit him ? "

" Clean through the face ! or, at any rate,

it looked like it," replied Savelsan, as Nare-Jones stood silent.

Harland shut the shutter and poked up the fire.

"It's a cursed creepy affair!" he said, "I hope the servants won't get hold of this nonsense. Ghosts play the very mischief with a house. Though I don't believe in them myself, he concluded."

Then Savelsan broke out in an unexpected place.

"Nor do I—as a rule," he said slowly. "Still you know it is a sickening idea to think of a spirit condemned to haunt the scene of its crime waiting for the world to die."

Harland and Nare-Jones looked at him.

"Have a whisky neat," suggested Harland, soothingly. "I never knew you taken that way before."

Nare-Jones laughed out. He says he does not know why he laughed nor why he said what follows.

"It's this way," he said. "The moment of foul satisfaction is gone for ever, yet for all time the guilty spirit must perpetuate its sin—the sin that brought no lasting reward, only a momentary reward experienced, it may be, centuries ago, but to which still clings the punishment of eternally rehearsing in loneliness, and cold, and gloom, the sin of other days. No punishment can be conceived more horrible. Savelsan is right."

"I think we've had enough about ghosts," said Harland, cheerfully, "let's go on. Hurry up, Savelsan."

"There's the billiard ball," said Nare-Jones. "Who'll go fetch?"

"Not I," replied Savelsan promptly. "When that—was at the window, I felt sick."

Nare-Jones nodded. "And I wanted to bolt!" he said emphatically.

Harland faced about from the fire.

"And I, though I saw nothing but the shutter, I—hang it!—don't yer know—so did I! There was panic in the air for a minute. But I'm shot if I'm afraid now," he concluded doggedly, "I'll go."

His heavy animal face was lit with courage and resolution.

"I've spent close upon five thousand pounds over this blessed house first and last, and I'm not going to be done out of it by any infernal spiritualism!" he added, as he took down his coat and pulled it on.

"It's all in view from the window except those few yards through the shrubbery," said Savelsan. "Take ·a stick and go. Though, on second thoughts, I bet you a fiver you don't."

"I don't want a stick," answered Harland. "I'm not afraid—not now—and I'd meet most men with my hands."

Nare-Jones opened the shutters again; the sash was low and he pushed the window up, and leant far out.

"It's not much of a drop," he said, and slung his legs out over the lintel; but the night was full of the smell, and something else. He leapt back into the room. "Don't go, Harland!"

Harland gave him a look that set his blood burning.

"What is there, after all, to be afraid of in a ghost?" he asked heavily.

Nare-Jones, sick with the sense of his own newly-born cowardice, yet entirely unable to master it, answered feebly :

" I can't say, but don't go."

The words seemed inevitable, though he could have kicked himself for hanging back.

There was a forced laugh from Savelsan.

" Give it up and stop at home, little man," he said.

Harland merely snorted in reply, and laid his great leg over the window ledge. The other two watched his big, tweed-clad figure as it crossed the grass and disappeared into the shrubbery.

" You and I are in a preposterous funk," said Savelsan, with unpleasant explicitness, as Harland, whistling loudly, passed into the shadow.

But this was a point on which Nare-Jones could not bring himself to speak at that moment. Then they sat on the sill and waited. The moon shone out clearly above the avenue, which now lay white and undimmed between its crowding trees.

" And he's whistling because he's afraid," continued Savelsan.

" He's not often afraid," replied Nare-Jones shortly ; " besides, he's doing what neither of us were very keen on."

The whistling stopped suddenly. Savelsan said afterwards that he fancied he saw Harland's huge, grey-clad shoulders, with uplifted arms, rise for a second above the bushes.

Then out of the silence came peal upon peal of that infernal laughter, and, following it, the thin pitiful crying of the child. That too ceased, and an absolute stillness seemed to fall upon the place.

They leant out and listened intently. The minutes passed slowly. In the middle of the avenue the billiard ball glinted on the gravel, but there was no sign of Harland emerging from the shrubbery path.

"He should be there by now," said Nare-Jones anxiously.

They listened again; everything was quiet. The ticking of Harland's big watch on the mantel-piece was distinctly audible.

"This is too much," said Nare-Jones. "I'm going to see where he is."

He swung himself out on the grass, and Savelsan called to him to wait, as he was coming also. While Nare-Jones stood waiting, there was a sound as of a pig grunting and rooting among the dead leaves in the shrubbery.

They ran forward into the darkness, and found the shrubbery path. A minute later they came upon something that tossed and snorted and rolled under the shrubs.

"Great Heavens!" cried Nare-Jones, "it's Harland!"

"He's breaking somebody's neck." added Savelsan, peering into the gloom.

Nare-Jones was himself again. The powerful instinct of his profession—the help-giving instinct, possessed him to the exclusion of every other feeling.

"He's in a fit—just a fit," he said in matter of fact tones, as he bent over the struggling form; "that's all."

With the assistance of Savelsan, he managed to carry Harland out into the open drive. Harland's eyes were fearful, and froth hung about his blue puffing lips as they laid him down upon the ground. He rolled over, and lay still, while from the shadows broke another shout of laughter.

"It's apoplexy. We must get him away from here," said Nare-Jones. "But, first, I'm going to see what is in those bushes."

He dashed through the shrubbery, backwards and forwards. He seemed to feel the strength of ten men as he wrenched and tore and trampled the branches, letting in the light of the moon to its darkness. At last he paused, exhausted.

"Of course, there's nothing," said Savelsan wearily. "What did you expect after the incident of the billiard ball ? "

Together, with awful toil, they bore the big man down the narrow avenue, and at the lodge gates they met the carriage.

Some time later the subject of their common experiences at Medhans Lea was discussed amongst the three men. Indeed, for many weeks Harland had not been in a state to discuss any subject at all, but as soon as he was allowed to do so, he invited Nare-Jones and Savelsan to meet Mr. Flaxman Low, the scientist, whose works on psychology and kindred matters are so well known at the Métropole, to thresh out the matter.

Flaxman Low listened with his usual air of gentle abstraction, from time to time making notes on the back of an envelope. He looked at each narrator in turn as he took up the thread of the story. He understood perfectly that the man who stood furthest from the mystery must inevitably have been the self-centred Savelsan; next in order came Nare-Jones, with sympathetic possibilities, but a crowded brain ; closest of all would be big, kindly Harland, with more than one strong animal instinct about him, and whose bulk of matter was evidently permeated by a receptive spirit.

When they had ended, Savelsan turned to Flaxman Low.

"There you have the events, Mr. Low. Now, the question is how to deal with them."

"Classify them," replied Flaxman Low.

"The crying would seem to indicate a child," began Savelsan, ticking off the list on his fingers ; "the black figure, the face at the window, and the laughter. are naturally connected. So far I can go alone. I conclude that we saw the apparition of a man, possibly a priest, who had during his lifetime illtreated a child, and whose punishment it is to haunt the scene of his crime."

"Precisely—the punishment being worked out under conditions which admit of human observation," returned Flaxman Low. "As for the child the sound of crying was merely part of the *mise-en-scène*. The child was not there."

"But that explanation stops short of several points. Now about the suggestive thoughts experienced by my friend, Nare-Jones ; what brought on the fit in the case of Mr. Harland, who assures us that he was not suffering from fright or other violent emotion ; and what connection can be traced between all these things and the Bengali idol ? " Savelsan ended.

"Let us take the Bengali idol first," said Low. "It is just one of those discrepant particulars which, at first sight, seem wholly irreconcilable with the rest of the phenomena, yet these often form a test point, by which our

theories are proved or otherwise." Flaxman
Low took up the metal calf from the table as he
spoke. " I should be inclined to connect this
with the child. Observe it. It has not been
roughly used ; it is rubbed and dinted as a play-
thing usually is. I should say the child may have
had Anglo-Indian relations."

At this, Nare-Jones bent forward, and in
his turn examined the idol, while Savelsan smiled
his thin, incredulous smile.

" These are ingenious theories," he said ; " but
we are really no nearer to facts, I am afraid."

" The only proof would be an inquiry into the
former history of Medhans Lea ; if events had
happened there which would go to support this
theory, why, then—— But I cannot supply that
information since I never heard of Medhans Lea
or the ghost until I entered this room."

" I know something of Medhans Lea," put
in Nare-Jones. " I found out a good deal about
it before I left the place. And I must congratulate Mr. Low on his methods, for his theory
tallies in a wonderful manner with the facts of
the case. The house was long known to be haunted.
It seems that many years ago a lady, the widow
of an Indian officer, lived there with her only child,
a boy, for whom she engaged a tutor, a dark-
looking man, who wore a long black coat like a
cassock, and was called ' the Jesuit ' by the
country people.

" One evening the man took the boy out into
the shrubbery. Screams were heard, and when
the child was brought in he was found to have
lost his reason. He used to cry and shriek
incessantly, but was never able to tell what had
been done to him as long as he lived. As for

this idol, the mother probably brought it with
her from India, and the child used it as a toy,
perhaps, because he was allowed no others.
Hullo!" In handling the calf, Nare-Jones had
touched some hidden spring, the head opened,
disclosing a small cavity, from which dropped a
little ring of blue beads, such as children make.
He held it up. "This affords good proof."

"Yes," admitted Savelsan grudgingly. "But
how about your sensations and Harland's
seizure? You must know what was done to
the child, Harland—what did you see in the
shrubbery?"

Harland's florid face assumed a queer pallor.

"I saw something," replied he hesitatingly,
"but I can't recall what it was. I only remember
being possessed by a blind terror, and then
nothing more until I recovered consciousness at
the hotel next day."

"Can you account for this, Mr. Low?" asked
Nare-Jones, "and there was also my strange
notion of the whispering in the avenue."

"I think so," replied Flaxman Low. "I
believe that the theory of atmospheric influences,
which includes the power of environment to re-
produce certain scenes and also thoughts, would
throw light upon your sensations as well as Mr.
Harland's. Such influences play a far larger
part in our everyday experience than we have
as yet any idea of."

There was a silence of a few moments; then
Harland spoke:

"I fancy that we have said all that there is to
be said upon the matter. We are much obliged
to you, Mr. Low. I don't know how it strikes
you other fellows, but, speaking for myself, I

have seen enough of ghosts to last me for a very
long time."

"And now," ended Harland wearily, "if you
have no objections, we will pass on to pleasanter
subjects."

III

THE STORY OF THE MOOR ROAD

" THE medical profession must always have its own peculiar offshoots," said Mr. Flaxman Low, " some are trades, some mere hobbies, others, again, are allied subjects of a serious and profound nature. Now, as a student of psychical phenomena, I account myself only two degrees removed from the ordinary general practitioner."

" How do you make that out ? " returned Colonel Daimley, pushing the decanter of old port invitingly across the table.

" The nerve and brain specialist is the link between myself and the man you would send for if you had a touch of lumbago," replied Low with a slight smile. " Each division is but a higher grade of the same ladder—a step upwards into the unknown. I consider that I stand just one step above the specialist who makes a study of brain disease and insanity ; he is at work on the disorders of the embodied spirit, while I deal with abnormal conditions of the free and detached spirit."

Colonel Daimley laughed aloud.

" That won't do, Low ! No, no ! First prove that your ghosts are sick."

D

"Certainly," replied Low gravely. "A very small proportion of spirits return as apparitions after the death of the body. Hence we may conclude that a ghost is a spirit in an abnormal condition. Abnormal conditions of the body usually indicate disease ; why not of the spirit also ? "

"That sounds fair enough," observed Lane Chaddam, the third man present. "Has the Colonel told you of our spook ? "

The Colonel shook his handsome grey head in some irritation.

"You haven't convinced me yet, Lane, that it is a spook," he said drily. "Human nature is at the bottom of most things in this world according to my opinion."

"What spook is this ? " asked Flaxman Low. "I heard nothing of it when I was down with you last year."

"It's a recent acquisition," replied Lane Chaddam. "I wish we were rid of it for my part."

"Have you seen it ? " asked Low as he relit his long pipe.

"Yes, and felt it ! "

"What is it ? "

"That's for you to say. He nearly broke my neck for me—that's all I can swear to."

Low knew Chaddam well. He was a long-limbed, athletic young fellow, with a good show of cups in his rooms, and was one of the various short-distance runners mentioned in the Bad-minton as having done the hundred in level time, and not the sort of man whose neck is easy to break.

"How did it happen ? " asked Flaxman Low.

"About a fortnight ago," replied Chaddam, "I was flight-shooting near the barn where the hounds killed the otter last year. When the light began to fail, I thought I would come home by the old quarry, and pot anything that showed itself. As I walked along the far bank of the burn, I saw a man on the near side standing on the patch of the sand below the reeds and watching me. As I came nearer I heard him coughing ; it sounded like a sick cow. He stood still as if waiting for me. I thought it odd, because amongst the meres and water-meadows down there one never meets a stranger."

"Could you see him pretty clearly ? "

"I saw his outline clearly, but not his face, because his back was toward the west. He was tall and jerry-built, so to speak, and had a little head no bigger than a child's, and he wore a fur cap with queer upstanding ears. When I came close, he suddenly slipped away ; he jumped behind a big dyke, and I lost sight of him. But I didn't pay much attention ; I had my gun, and I concluded it was a tramp."

"Tramps don't follow men of your size," observed Low with a smile.

"This fellow did, at any rate. When I got across to the spot where he had been standing— the sand is soft there—I looked for his tracks. I knew he was bound to have a big foot of his own considering his height. But there were no footprints ! "

"No footprints ? You mean it was too dark for you to see them ? " broke in Colonel Daimley.

"I am sure I should have seen them had there been any," persisted Chaddam quietly. "Besides, a man can't take a leap as he did without leaving a good hole behind him. The sand was perfectly smooth, because there had been a strong east wind all day. I looked about and seeing no marks, I went on to the top of the knoll above the quarry. After a bit I felt I was followed, though I couldn't see anyone. You remember the thorn bush that overhangs the quarry pool ? I stopped there and bent over the edge of the cliff to see if there was anything in the pool. As I stooped I felt a point like a steel puncheon catch me in the small of the back. I kicked off from the quarry wall as well as I could, so as to avoid the broken rocks below, and I just managed to clear them, but I fell into the water with a flop that knocked the wind out of me. However, I held on to the gun, and, after a minute, I climbed to a ledge under the cliff and waited to see what my friend on top would do next. He waited, too. I couldn't see him, but I heard him—he coughed up there in the dusk, the most ghastly noise I ever heard. The Colonel laughs at me, but it was about as nasty a half-hour as I care to have. In the end, I swam out across the pool and got home."

"I laugh at Lane," said the Colonel, "but all the same, it's a bad spot for a fall."

"You say he struck you in the back ? " asked Flaxman Low, turning to Chaddam.

"Yes, and his finger was like a steel punch."

"What does Mrs. Daimley say to this affair ? " went on Low presently.

"Not a word to my wife or Olivia, my dear Low ! " exclaimed Colonel Daimley. "It would frighten them needlessly ; besides, there would be an infernal fuss if we wanted to go flighting or anything after dark. I only fear for them, as

they often drive into Nerbury by the Moor Road,
which passes close by the quarry."

" Do they go in for their letters every evening
as they used to do ? "

" Just the same.   And they won't take Stubbs
with them, in spite of advice."   The Colonel
looked disconsolately at Low.   "Women are
angels, bless them ! but they are the dickens to
deal with because they always want to know
why ? "

" And now, Low, what have you to say about
it ? " asked Chaddam.

" Have you told me all ? "

" Yes.   The only other thing is that Livy says
she hears someone coughing in the spinney most
nights."

" If all is as you say, Chaddam—pardon me,
but in cases like this imagination is apt to play an
unsuspected part—I should think that you
have come upon a unique experience.   What
you have told me is not to be explained upon the
lines of any ordinary theory."

After this they followed the ladies into the
drawing-room, where they found Mrs. Daimley
immersed in a novel as usual, and Livy looking
pretty enough to account for the frequent
presence of Lane Chaddam at Low Riddings.
He was a distant cousin of the Colonel, and took
advantage of his relationship to pay protracted
visits to Northumberland.

Some years previous to the date of the above
events, Colonel Daimley had bought and enlarged
a substantial farmhouse which stood in a dip
south of a lonely sweep of Northumbrian moors.
It was a land of pale blue skies and far off fringes
of black and ragged pine trees.

From the house a lane led over the wind-
swept shoulder of the upland down to a hollow
spanned by a railway bridge, then up again
across the high levels of the moors until at length
it lost itself in the outskirts of the little town of
Nerbury. This Moor Road was peculiarly lonely :
it approached but one cottage the whole way,
and ran very nearly over the doorstep of that one
—a deserted-looking slip of a place between the
railway bridge and the quarry. Beyond the
quarry stretched acres of marshland, meadows
and reedy meres, all of which had been manipu-
lated with such ability by the Colonel, that the
duck shooting on his land was the envy of the
neighbourhood.

In spite of its loneliness the Moor Road was
much frequented by the Daimleys, who preferred
it to the high road, which was uninteresting and
much longer. Mrs. Daimley and Olivia drove
in of an evening to fetch their letters—being
people with nothing on earth to do, they were
naturally always in a hurry to get their letters—
and they perpetually had parcels waiting for them
at the station which required to be called for at
all sorts of hours. Thus it will be seen that the
fact of the quarry being haunted by Lane
Chaddam's assailant, formed a very real danger
to the inhabitants of Low Riddings.

At breakfast next day Livy said the tramp
had been coughing in the spinney half the night.

" In what direction ? " asked Flaxman Low.

Livy pointed to the window which looked on
to the gate and the thick boundary hedge, the
last still full of crisp ruddy leaves.

" You feel an interest in your tramp, Miss
Daimley ? "

"Of course, poor creature! I wanted to go out to look for him the other night, but they would not allow me."

"That was before we knew he was so interesting," said Chaddam. "I promise we'll catch him for you next time he comes."

And this was in fact the programme they tried to carry out, but although the coughing was heard in the spinney, no one even caught a glimpse of any living thing moving or hiding among the trees.

The next stage of the affair happened to be an experience of Livy's. In some excitement she told the assembled family at dinner that she had just seen the coughing tramp.

Lane Chaddam changed colour.

"You don't mean to say, Livy, that you went to search for him alone?" he exclaimed half-angrily.

Flaxman Low and the Colonel wisely went on eating oyster patties without taking any apparent notice of the girl's news.

"Why shouldn't I?" asked Livy quickly; "but as it happens I saw him in Scully's cottage by the quarry this evening."

"What?" said Colonel Daimley, "in Scully's cottage. I'll see to that."

"Why? Are you all so prejudiced against my poor tramp!"

"On the contrary," replied Flaxman Low, "we all want to know what he's like."

"So odd-looking! I was driving home alone from the post when, as I passed the quarry cottage, I heard the cough. You know it is quite unmistakable; I looked up at the window and there he was. I have never seen anybody in the least like him. His face is ghastly pale and perfectly

hairless, and he has such a little head. He stared
at me so threateningly that I whipped up Lorelie."

" Were you frightened, then ? "

" Not exactly, but he had such a wicked face
that I drove away as fast as I could."

" I understood that you had arranged to send
Stubbs for the letters ? " said Colonel Daimley
with some annoyance. " Why can't girls say
what they mean ? "

Livy made no reply, and after a pause Chaddam
put a question.

" You must have passed along the Moor Road
about seven o'clock ? "

" Yes, it was after six when I left the Post
Office," replied Livy. " Why ? "

" It was quite dark—how did you see the hairless man so plainly ? I was round on the marshes
all the evening, and I am quite certain there
was no light at any time in Scully's cottage."

" I don't remember whether there was any
light behind him in the room," returned Livy
after a moment's consideration ; " I only know
that I saw his head and face quite plainly."

There was no more said on the subject at the
time, though the Colonel forbade Livy to run
any further risks by going alone on the Moor Road.
After this the three men paraded the lane and
lay in wait for the hairless tramp or ghost. On
the second evening their watch was rewarded,
when Chaddam came hurriedly into the smoking-
room to say that the coughing could at that
instant be heard in the hedge by the dining-room.
It was still early, although the evening had
closed in with clouds, and all outside was dark.

" I'll deal with him this time effectually ! "
exclaimed the Colonel. " I'll slip out the back

way, and lie in the hedge down the road by the field gate. You two must chivy him out to me, and when he comes along, I'll have him against the sky-line and give him a charge of No. 4 if he shows fight."

The Colonel stole down the lane while the others beat the spinney and hedge, Flaxman Low very much chagrined at being forced to deal with an interesting problem in this rough and ready fashion. However, he saw that on this occasion at least it would be useless to oppose the Colonel's notions. When he and Chaddam met after beating the hedge they saw a tall figure shamble away rapidly down the lane towards the Colonel's hiding-place.

They stood still and waited for developments, but the minutes followed each other in intense stillness. Then they went to find the Colonel.

" Hullo, Colonel, anything wrong ? " asked Chaddam on nearing the field gate.

The Colonel straightened himself with the help of Chaddam's arm.

" Did you see him ? " he whispered.

" We thought so. Why did you not fire ? "

" Because," said the Colonel in a husky voice, "I had no gun ! "

" But you took it with you ? "

" Yes."

Flaxman Low opened the lantern he carried, and, as the light swept round in a wide circle, something glinted on the grass. It was the stock of the Colonel's gun. A little further off they came upon the Damascus barrels bent and twisted into a ball like so much fine wire. Presently the Colonel explained.

" I saw him coming and meant to meet him,

but I seemed dazed—I couldn't move ! The gun
was snatched from me, and I made no resistance
—I don't know why." He took the gun-barrels
and examined them slowly. "I give in, Low,
no human hand did that."

During dinner Flaxman Low said abruptly :
"I suspect you have lately had an earthquake
down here."

"How did you know ? " asked Livy. "Have
you been to the quarry ? "

Low said he had not.

"It was such a poor little earthquake that
even the papers did not think it worth while to
mention it ! " went on Livy. "We didn't feel
any shock, and, in fact, knew nothing about it
until Dr. Petterped told us."

"You had a landslip though ? " went on Low.

Livy opened her pretty eyes.

"But you know all about it," she said. "Yes,
the landslip was just by the old quarry."

"I should like to see the place to-morrow,"
observed Low.

Next day, therefore, when the Colonel went off
to the coverts with a couple of neighbours, whom
he had invited to join him, Flaxman Low accompanied Chaddam to examine the scene of the
landslip.

From the edge of the upland, looking across
the hollow crowded with reedy pools, they could
see in the torn, reddish flank of the opposite
slope the sharp tilt of the broken strata. To
the right of this lay the old quarry, and about
a hundred yards to the left the lonely house and
the curving road.

Low descended into the hollow and spent a
long time in the spongy ground between the back

of the quarry and the lower edge of the newly-
uncovered strata, using his little hammer freely,
especially about one narrow black fissure, round
which he sniffed and pottered in absorbed silence.
Presently he called to Chaddam.

"There has been a slight explosion of gas—
a rare gas, here," he said. "I hardly hoped to
find traces of it, but it is unmistakable."

"Very unmistakable," agreed Chaddam, with
a laugh. "You'd have said so had you been
here when it happened."

"Ah, very satisfactory indeed. And that was
a fortnight ago, you say?"

"Rather more now. It took place a couple
of days before my fall into the quarry pool."

"Anyone ill near by—at that cottage for
instance?" asked Low, as he joined Chaddam.

"Why? Was that gas poisonous? There's
a man in the Colonel's employ named Scully in
that cottage, who has had pneumonia, but he was
on the mend when the landslip occurred. Since
then he has grown steadily worse."

"Is there anyone with him?"

"Yes, the Daimleys sent for a woman to look
after him. Scully's a very decent man. I often
go in to see him."

"And so does the hairless man apparently,"
added Low.

"No, that's the queer part of it. Neither he
nor the woman in charge have ever seen such a
person as Livy described. I don't know what to
think."

"The first thing to be done is to get the man
from here at once," said Low decidedly. "Let's
go in and see him."

They found Scully low and drowsy. The nurse

shook her head at the two visitors in a despondent
way.

"He grows weaker day by day," she said.

"Get him away from here at once," repeated
Low, as they went out.

"We might have him up at Low Riddings, but
he seems almost too weak to be moved," replied
Chaddam doubtfully.

"My dear fellow, it's his only chance of
life."

The Daimleys made arrangements for the
reception of Scully, provided Dr. Thomson of
Nerbury gave his consent to the removal. In the
afternoon, therefore, Chaddam bicycled into
Nerbury to see the doctor on the subject.

"If I were you, Chaddam," said Low before
he started, "I'd be back by daylight."

Unfortunately Dr. Thomson was on his rounds,
and did not return until after dark, by which
time it was too late to remove Scully that evening.
After leaving the doctor's house Chaddam went
to the station to inquire about a box from Mudie's.
The books having arrived, he took out a couple
of volumes for Mrs. Daimley's present consump-
tion, and was strapping them on in front of his
bicycle, when it struck him that unless he went
home by the Moor Road he would be late for
dinner.

Accordingly he branched off into the bare
track which led over the moors. The twilight
had deepened into a fine, cold night, and a moon
was swinging up into a pale, clear sky. The
spread of heather, purple in the daytime, appeared
jet black by moonlight, and across it he could
see the white ribbon of road stretching ahead
into the distance. The scents of the night were

fresh in his nostrils, as he ran easily along the level with the breeze behind him.

He soon reached the incline past Scully's cottage. Well away to the left lay the quarry pool like a blotch of ink under its shadowing cliff. There was no light in the cottage, and it seemed even more deserted-looking than usual.

As Chaddam flashed under the bridge, he heard a cough, and glanced back over his shoulder.

A tall, loose-jointed form he had seen once before, was rearing itself up upon the railway bridge. There was something curiously unhuman about the lank outlines and the cant of the small head with its prick-eared cap showing out so clearly against the lighter sky behind.

When Chaddam looked again, he saw the thing on the bridge fling up its long arms and leap down on to the road some thirty feet below.

Then Chaddam rode. He began to think he had been a fool to come, and he counted that he was a good mile from home. At first he fancied he heard footfalls, then he fancied there were none. The hard road flew under him, all thoughts of economising his strength were lost, his single aim was to make the pace.

Suddenly his bicycle jerked violently, and he was shot over into the road. As he fell, he turned his head and was conscious of a little, bleached, bestial face, wet with fury, not ten yards behind !

He sprang to his feet, and ran up the road as he had never run before. He ran wonderfully, but he might as well have tried to race a cheetah. It was not a question of speed, the game was in the hands of this thing with the limbs of a starved Hercules, whose bony knees seemed to leap into its ghastly face at every stride. Chaddam topped the slope with a sickening sense of his own power-lessness. Already he saw Low Riddings in the distance, and a dim light came creeping along the road towards him. Another frantic spurt, and he had almost reached the light, when a hand closed like a vice on his shoulder, and seemed to fasten on the flesh. He rushed blindly on towards the house. He saw the door-handle gleam, and in another second he had pitched head foremost on to the knotted matting in the hall.

When he recovered his senses, his first question was : " Where is Low ? "

" Didn't you meet him ? " asked Livy. " I —that is, we were anxious about you as you were so late, and I was just going to meet you when Mr. Low came downstairs and insisted on going instead."

Chaddam stood up.

" I must follow him."

But as he spoke the front door opened, and Flaxman Low entered, and looked up at the clock.

" Eight-twenty," he said. " You're late, Chaddam."

Afterwards in the smoking-room he gave an account of what he had seen.

" I saw Chaddam racing up the road with a tall figure behind him. It stretched out its hand and grasped his shoulder. The next instant it stopped short as if it had been shot. It seemed to reel back and collapse, and then limped off into the hedge like a disappointed dog."

Chaddam stood up and began to take off his coat.

" Whatever the thing is, it is something out of the common. Look here ! " he said, turning up his shirt sleeve over the point of his shoulder, where three singular marks were visible, irregularly placed as the fingers of a hand might fall. They were oblong in shape, about the size of a bean, and swollen in purple lumps well above the surface of the skin.

"Looks as if someone had been using a small cupping glass on you," remarked the Colonel uneasily. "What do you say to it, Low?"

"I say that since Chaddam has escaped with his life, I have only to congratulate him on what, in Europe certainly, is a unique adventure."

The Colonel threw his cigar into the fire.

"Such adventures are too dangerous for my taste," he said. "This creature has on two occasions murderously attacked Lane Chaddam, and it would, no doubt, have attacked Livy if it had had the chance. We must leave this place at once, or we shall be murdered in our beds!"

"I don't think, Colonel, that you will be troubled with this mysterious visitant again," replied Flaxman Low.

"Why not? Who or what is this horrible thing?"

"I believe it to be an Elemental Earth Spirit," returned Low. "No other solution fits the facts of the case."

"What is an Elemental?" resumed the Colonel irritably. "Remember, Low, I expect you to prove your theories so that a plain man may understand, if I am to stay on at Low Riddings."

"Eastern occultists describe wandering tribes of earth spirits evil intelligences, possessing spirit as distinct from soul—all inimical to man."

"But how do you know that the thing on the Moor Road is an Elemental?"

"Because the points of resemblance are curiously remarkable. The occultists say that when these spirits materialise, they appear in grotesque and uncouth forms ; secondly, that they are invariably bloodless and hairless ; thirdly, they move with extraordinary rapidity, and leave no footprints ; and, lastly, their agility and strength is superhuman. All these peculiarities have been observed in connection with the figure on the Moor Road."

"I admit that no man I have ever met with," commented Colonel Daimley, " could jump uninjured from a height of 30 ft., race a bicycle, and twist up gun-barrels like so much soft paper. So perhaps you're right. But can you tell me why or how it came here ? "

"My conclusions," began Low, "may seem to you far-fetched and ridiculous, but you must give them the benefit of the fact that they precisely account for the otherwise unaccountable features which mark this affair. I connect this appearance with the earthquake and the sick man."

"What ? Scully in league with the devil ? " exclaimed the Colonel bluntly. "Why, the man is too weak to leave his bed ; besides, he is a short, thick-set fellow, entirely unlike our haunting friend."

"You mistake me, Colonel," said Low, in his quiet tones. "These Elementals cannot take form without drawing upon the resources of the living. They absorb the vitality of any ailing person until it is exhausted, and the person dies."

"Then they begin operations upon a fresh victim ? A pleasant look-out to know we keep a well-attested vampire in the neighbourhood ! "

"Vampires are a distinct race, with different methods; one being that the Elemental is a wanderer, and goes far afield to search for a new victim."

"But why should it want to kill me?" put in Chaddam.

"As I have told you, they are animated solely by a blind malignity to the human race, and you happened to be handy."

"But the earthquake, Low; where is the connection there?" demanded the Colonel, with the air of a man who intends to corner his opponent.

Flaxman Low lit one cigar at the end of another before he replied.

"At this point," he said, "my own theories and observations and those of the old occultists overlap. The occultists held that some of these spirits are imprisoned in the interior of the earth, but may be set free in consequence of those shiftings and disturbances which take place during an earthquake. This in more modern language simply means that Elementals are in some manner connected with certain of the primary strata. Now, my own researches have led me to conclude that atmospheric influences are intimately associated with spiritual phenomena. Some gases appear to be productive of such phenomena. One of these is generated when certain of the primary formations are newly exposed to the common air."

"This is almost beyond belief—I don't understand you," said the Colonel.

"I am sorry that I cannot give you all the links in my own chain of reasoning," returned Low. "Much is still obscure, but the evidence is sufficiently strong to convince me that in such a

E

case of earthquake and landslip as has lately
taken place here the phenomenon of an embodied
Elemental might possibly be expected to follow,
given the one necessary adjunct of a sick person
in the near neighbourhood of the disturbance."

"But when this brute got hold of me, why
didn't it finish me off ? " asked Chaddam.   " Or
was it your coming that prevented it ? "

Flaxman Low considered.

"No, I don't think I can flatter myself that
my coming had anything to do with your escape.
It was a near thing—how near you will understand
when we hear further news of Scully in the
morning."

A servant entered the room at this moment.

"The woman has come up from the cottage,
sir, to say that Scully is dead."

"At what hour did he die ? " asked Low.

"About ten minutes past eight, sir, she says."

"The hour agrees exactly," commented Low,
when the man had left the room.   "The figure
stopped and collapsed so suddenly that I believed
something of this kind must have happened."

"But surely this is a very unprecedented
occurrence ? "

"It is," said Flaxman Low.   "Yet I can assure
you that if you take the trouble to glance through
the pages of the psychical periodicals you will
find many statements at least as wonderful."

"But are they true ? "

Flaxman Low shrugged his shoulders.

"At any rate," said he, "we know this is."

The Daimleys have spent many pleasant days
at Low Riddings since then, but Chaddam—who
has acquired a right to control Miss Livy's actions
more or less—persists in his objection to any

solitary expeditions to Nerbury along the Moor Road. For, although the figure has never been seen about Low Riddings since, some strange stories have lately appeared in the papers of a similar mysterious figure which has been met with more than once in the lonelier spots about North London. If it be true that this nameless wandering spirit, with the strength and activity of twenty men, still haunts our lonely roads, the sooner Mr. Flaxman Low exorcises it the better.

IV

THE STORY OF BAELBROW

IT is a matter for regret that so many of Mr.
Flaxman Low's reminiscences should deal with
the darker episodes of his experiences. Yet this
is almost unavoidable, as the more purely
scientific and less strongly marked cases would
not, perhaps, contain the same elements of interest for the general public, however valuable and
instructive they might be to the expert student.
It has also been considered better to choose the
completer cases, those that ended in something
like satisfactory proof, rather than the many
instances where the thread broke off abruptly
amongst surmisings, which it was never possible
to subject to convincing tests.

North of a low-lying strip of country on the
East Anglian coast, the promontory of Bael
Ness thrusts out a blunt nose into the sea.
On the Ness, backed by pinewoods, stands a
square, comfortable stone mansion, known to
the countryside as Baelbrow. It has faced the
east winds for close upon three hundred years,
and during the whole period has been the home
of the Swaffam family, who were never in anywise
put out of conceit of their ancestral dwelling

by the fact that it had always been haunted.
Indeed, the Swaffams were proud of the Baelbrow
Ghost, which enjoyed a wide notoriety, and no
one dreamt of complaining of its behaviour
until Professor Van der Voort of Louvain laid
information against it, and sent an urgent appeal
for help to Mr. Flaxman Low.

The Professor, who was well acquainted with
Mr. Low, detailed the circumstances of his ten-
ancy of Baelbrow, and the unpleasant events
that had followed thereupon.

It appeared that Mr. Swaffam, senior, who
spent a large portion of his time abroad, had
offered to lend his house to the Professor for the
summer season. When the Van der Voorts
arrived at Baelbrow, they were charmed with the
place. The prospect, though not very varied,
was at least extensive, and the air exhilarating.
Also the Professor's daughter enjoyed frequent
visits from her betrothed—Harold Swaffam—
and the Professor was delightfully employed in
overhauling the Swaffam library.

The Van der Voorts had been duly told of the
ghost, which lent distinction to the old house,
but never in any way interfered with the comfort
of the inmates. For some time they found this
description to be strictly true, but with the
beginning of October came a change. Up to this
time and as far back as the Swaffam annals
reached, the ghost had been a shadow, a rustle, a
passing sigh—nothing definite or troublesome.
But early in October strange things began to
occur, and the terror culminated when a house-
maid was found dead in a corridor three weeks
later. Upon this the Professor felt that it was
time to send for Flaxman Low.

Mr. Low arrived upon a chilly evening when
the house was already beginning to blur in the
purple twilight, and the resinous scent of the pines
came sweetly on the land breeze. Van der
Voort welcomed him in the spacious, fire-lit hall.
He was a stout man with a quantity of white
hair, round eyes emphasised by spectacles, and
a kindly, dreamy face. His life-study was
philology, and his two relaxations chess and the
smoking of a big bowled meerschaum.

"Now, Professor," said Mr. Low when they
had settled themselves in the smoking-room,
"how did it all begin?"

"I will tell you," replied Van der Voort,
thrusting out his chin, and tapping his broad
chest, and speaking as if an unwarrantable liberty
had been taken with him. "First of all, it has
shown itself to me!"

Mr. Flaxman Low smiled and assured him
that nothing could be more satisfactory.

"But not at all satisfactory!" exclaimed
the Professor. "I was sitting here alone, it
might have been midnight—when I hear something come creeping like a little dog with its
nails, tick-tick, upon the oak flooring of the hall.
I whistle, for I think it is the little 'Rags' of
my daughter, and afterwards opened the door,
and I saw "—he hesitated and looked hard at
Low through his spectacles, "something that was
just disappearing into the passage which connects
the two wings of the house. It was a figure,
not unlike the human figure, but narrow and
straight. I fancied I saw a bunch of black hair,
and a flutter of something detached, which may
have been a handkerchief. I was overcome by
a feeling of repulsion. I heard a few clicking

steps, then it stopped, as I thought, at the museum door. Come, I will show you the spot."

The Professor conducted Mr. Low into the hall. The main staircase, dark and massive, yawned above them, and directly behind it ran the passage referred to by the Professor. It was over twenty feet long, and about midway led past a deep arch containing a door reached by two steps. Van der Voort explained that this door formed the entrance to a large room called the Museum, in which Mr. Swaffam, senior, who was something of a dilettante, stored the various curios he picked up during his excursions abroad. The Professor went on to say that he immediately followed the figure, which he believed had gone into the museum, but he found nothing there except the cases containing Swaffam's treasures.

"I mentioned my experience to no one. I concluded that I had seen the ghost. But two days after, one of the female servants coming through the passage, in the dark, declared that a man leapt out at her from the embrasure of the Museum door, but she released herself and ran screaming into the servants' hall. We at once made a search but found nothing to substantiate her story.

"I took no notice of this, though it coincided pretty well with my own experience. The week after, my daughter Lena came down late one night for a book. As she was about to cross the hall, something leapt upon her from behind. Women are of little use in serious investigations —she fainted ! Since then she has been ill and the doctor says ' Run down.' " Here the

Professor spread out his hands. " So she leaves for
a change to-morrow. Since then other members
of the household have been attacked in much
the same manner, with always the same result,
they faint and are weak and useless when they
recover.

" But, last Wednesday, the affair became a
tragedy. By that time the servants had refused
to come through the passage except in a crowd
of three or four,—most of them preferring to go
round by the terrace to reach this part of the
house. But one maid, named Eliza Freeman,
said she was not afraid of the Baelbrow Ghost,
and undertook to put out the lights in the hall
one night. When she had done so, and was
returning through the passage past the Museum
door, she appears to have been attacked, or at
any rate frightened. In the grey of the morning
they found her lying beside the steps dead. There
was a little blood upon her sleeve but no mark
upon her body except a small raised pustule
under the ear. The doctor said the girl was
extraordinarily anæmic, and that she probably
died from fright, her heart being weak. I was
surprised at this, for she had always seemed
to be a particularly strong and active young
woman."

" Can I see Miss Van der Voort to-morrow
before she goes ? " asked Low, as the Professor
signified he had nothing more to tell.

The Professor was rather unwilling that his
daughter should be questioned, but he at last gave
his permission, and next morning Low had a
short talk with the girl before she left the house.
He found her a very pretty girl, though listless
and startlingly pale, and with a frightened stare

in her light brown eyes. Mr. Low asked if she
could describe her assailant.

"No," she answered. "I could not see him
for he was behind me. I only saw a dark, bony
hand, with shining nails, and a bandaged arm
pass just under my eyes before I fainted."

"Bandaged arm? I have heard nothing of
this."

"Tut—tut, mere fancy!" put in the Professor
impatiently.

"I saw the bandages on the arm," repeated
the girl, turning her head wearily away, "and I
smelt the antiseptics it was dressed with."

"You have hurt your neck," remarked Mr.
Low, who noticed a small circular patch of pink
under her ear.

She flushed and paled, raising her hand to her
neck with a nervous jerk, as she said in a low
voice:

"It has almost killed me. Before he touched
me, I knew he was there! I felt it!"

When they left her the Professor apologised
for the unreliability of her evidence, and pointed
out the discrepancy between her statement and
his own.

"She says she sees nothing but an arm, yet
I tell you it had no arms! Preposterous!
Conceive a wounded man entering this house
to frighten the young women! I do not know
what to make of it! Is it a man, or is it the
Baelbrow Ghost?"

During the afternoon when Mr. Low and the
Professor returned from a stroll on the shore,
they found a dark-browed young man with a
bull neck, and strongly marked features, standing

sullenly before the hall fire. The Professor presented him to Mr. Low as Harold Swaffam.

Swaffam seemed to be about thirty, but was already known as a far-seeing and successful member of the Stock Exchange.

"I am pleased to meet you, Mr. Low," he began, with a keen glance, "though you don't look sufficiently high-strung for one of your profession."

Mr. Low merely bowed.

"Come, you don't defend your craft against my insinuations?" went on Swaffam. "And so you have come to rout out our poor old ghost from Baelbrow? You forget that he is an heir-loom, a family possession! What's this about his having turned rabid, eh, Professor?" he ended, wheeling round upon Van der Voort in his brusque way.

The Professor told the story over again. It was plain that he stood rather in awe of his prospective son-in-law.

"I heard much the same from Lena, whom I met at the station," said Swaffam. "It is my opinion that the women in this house are suffering from an epidemic of hysteria. You agree with me, Mr. Low?"

"Possibly. Though hysteria could hardly account for Freeman's death."

"I can't say as to that until I have looked further into the particulars. I have not been idle since I arrived. I have examined the Museum. No one has entered it from the out-side, and there is no other way of entrance except through the passage. The flooring is laid, I happen to know, on a thick layer of concrete. And there the case for the ghost stands at present."

After a few moments of dogged reflection, he swung round on Mr. Low, in a manner that seemed peculiar to him when about to address any person. "What do you say to this plan, Mr. Low ? I propose to drive the Professor over to Ferryvale, to stop there for a day or two at the hotel, and I will also dispose of the servants who still remain in the house for, say, forty-eight hours. Meanwhile you and I can try to go further into the secret of the ghost's new pranks ? "

Flaxman Low replied that this scheme exactly met his views, but the Professor protested against being sent away. Harold Swaffam, however, was a man who liked to arrange things in his own fashion, and within forty-five minutes he and Van der Voort departed in the dogcart.

The evening was lowering, and Baelbrow, like all houses built in exposed situations, was extremely susceptible to the changes of the weather. Therefore, before many hours were over, the place was full of creaking noises as the screaming gale battered at the shuttered windows, and the tree-branches tapped and groaned against the walls.

Harold Swaffam on his way back, was caught in the storm and drenched to the skin. It was, therefore, settled that after he had changed his clothes he should have a couple of hours' rest on the smoking-room sofa, while Mr. Low kept watch in the hall.

The early part of the night passed over uneventfully. A light burned faintly in the great wainscotted hall, but the passage was dark. There was nothing to be heard but the wild moan and whistle of the wind coming in from the sea, and the squalls of rain dashing against the windows.

As the hours advanced, Mr. Low lit a lantern that lay at hand, and, carrying it along the passage tried the Museum door. It yielded, and the wind came muttering through to meet him. He looked round at the shutters and behind the big cases which held Mr. Swaffam's treasures, to make sure that the room contained no living occupant but himself.

Suddenly he fancied he heard a scraping noise behind him, and turned round, but discovered nothing to account for it. Finally, he laid the lantern on a bench so that its light should fall through the door into the passage, and returned again to the hall, where he put out the lamp, and then once more took up his station by the closed door of the smoking-room.

A long hour passed, during which the wind continued to roar down the wide hall chimney, and the old boards creaked as if furtive footsteps were gathering from every corner of the house. But Flaxman Low heeded none of these ; he was awaiting for a certain sound.

After a while, he heard it—the cautious scraping of wood on wood. He leant forward to watch the Museum door. Click, click, came the curious dog-like tread upon the tiled floor of the Museum, till the thing, whatever it was, paused and listened behind the open door. The wind lulled at the moment, and Low listened also, but no further sound was to be heard, only slowly across the broad ray of light falling through the door grew a stealthy shadow.

Again the wind rose, and blew in heavy gusts about the house, till even the flame in the lantern flickered ; but when it steadied once more, Flaxman Low saw that the silent form had passed

through the door, and was now on the steps
outside. He could just make out a dim shadow
in the dark angle of the embrasure.

Presently, from the shapeless shadow came a
sound Mr. Low was not prepared to hear. The
thing sniffed the air with the strong, audible inspir-
ation of a bear, or some large animal. At the
same moment, carried on the draughts of the hall,
a faint, unfamiliar odour reached his nostrils.
Lena Van der Voort's words flashed back upon
him—this, then, was the creature with the bandaged arm !

Again, as the storm shrieked and shook the
windows, a darkness passed across the light.
The thing had sprung out from the angle of the
door, and Flaxman Low knew that it was making
its way towards him through the illusive blackness of the hall. He hesitated for a second ; then
he opened the smoking-room door.

Harold Swaffam sat up on the sofa, dazed
with sleep.

" What has happened ? Has it come ? "

Low told him what he had just seen. Swaffam
listened half-smilingly.

" What do you make of it now ? " he said.

" I must ask you to defer that question for a
little," replied Low.

" Then you. mean me to suppose that you
have a theory to fit all these incongruous items ? "

" I have a theory, which may be modified by
further knowledge," said Low. " Meantime, am
I right in concluding from the name of this house
that it was built on a barrow or burying-place ? "

" You are right, though that has nothing to
do with the latest freaks of our ghost," returned
Swaffam decidedly.

"I also gather that Mr. Swaffam has lately sent home one of the many cases now lying in the Museum ? " went on Mr. Low.

" He sent one, certainly, last September."

" And you have opened it," asserted Low.

" Yes ; though I flattered myself I had left no trace of my handiwork."

" I have not examined the cases," said Low. "I inferred that you had done so from other facts."

"Now, one thing more," went on Swaffam, still smiling. " Do you imagine there is any danger—I mean to men like ourselves ? Hysterical women cannot be taken into serious account."

" Certainly ; the gravest danger to any person who moves about this part of the house alone after dark," replied Low.

Harold Swaffam leant back and crossed his legs.

" To go back to the beginning of our conversation, Mr. Low, may I remind you of the various conflicting particulars you will have to reconcile before you can present any decent theory to the world ? "

" I am quite aware of that."

" First of all, our original ghost was a mere misty presence, rather guessed at from vague sounds and shadows—now we have a something that is tangible, and that can, as we have proof, kill with fright. Next Van der Voort declares the thing was a narrow, long and distinctly armless object, while Miss Van der Voort has not only seen the arm and hand of a human being, but saw them clearly enough to tell us that the nails were gleaming and the arm bandaged,

She also felt its strength. Van der Voort, on the other hand, maintained that it clicked along like a dog—you bear out this description with the additional information that it sniffs like a wild beast. Now what can this thing be ? It is capable of being seen, smelt, and felt, yet it hides itself, successfully in a room where there is no cavity or space sufficient to afford covert to a cat ! You still tell me that you believe that you can explain ? "

" Most certainly," replied Flaxman Low with conviction.

" I have not the slightest intention or desire to be rude, but as a mere matter of common sense, I must express my opinion plainly. I believe the whole thing to be the result of excited imaginations, and I am about to prove it. Do you think there is any further danger to-night ? "

" Very great danger to-night," replied Low.

" Very well ; as I said, I am going to prove it. I will ask you to allow me to lock you up in one of the distant rooms, where I can get no help from you, and I will pass the remainder of the night walking about the passage and hall in the dark. That should give proof one way or the other."

" You can do so if you wish, but I must at least beg to be allowed to look on. I will leave the house and watch what goes on from the window in the passage, which I saw opposite the Museum door. You cannot, in any fairness, refuse to let me be a witness."

" I cannot, of course," returned Swaffam. " Still, the night is too bad to turn a dog out into, and I warn you that I shall lock you out."

" That will not matter. Lend me a macintosh,

and leave the lantern lit in the Museum, where I
placed it."

Swaffam agreed to this. Mr. Low gives a
graphic account of what followed. He left
the house and was duly locked out, and, after
groping his way round the house, found himself
at length outside the window of the passage,
which was almost opposite to the door of the
Museum. The door was still ajar and a thin
band of light cut out into the gloom. Further
down the hall gaped black and void. Low,
sheltering himself as well as he could from the
rain, waited for Swaffam's appearance. Was
the terrible yellow watcher balancing itself upon
its lean legs in the dim corner opposite, ready
to spring out with its deadly strength upon the
passer-by ?

Presently Low heard a door bang inside the
house, and the next moment Swaffam appeared
with a candle in his hand, an isolated spread
of weak rays against the vast darkness behind.
He advanced steadily down the passage, his dark
face grim and set, and as he came Mr. Low
experienced that tingling sensation, which is
so often the forerunner of some strange experience.
Swaffam passed on towards the other end of
the passage. There was a quick vibration of
the Museum door as a lean shape with a shrunken
head leapt out into the passage after him. Then
all together came a hoarse shout, the noise of a
fall and utter darkness.

In an instant, Mr. Low had broken the glass,
opened the window, and swung himself into the
passage. There he lit a match and as it flared
he saw by its dim light a picture painted for a
second upon the obscurity beyond.

Swaffam's big figure lay with outstretched arms, face downwards, and as Low looked a crouching shape extricated itself from the fallen man, raising a narrow vicious head from his shoulder.

The match spluttered feebly and went out, and Low heard a flying step click on the boards, before he could find the candle Swaffam had dropped. Lighting it, he stooped over Swaffam and turned him on his back. The man's strong colour had gone, and the wax-white face looked whiter still against the blackness of hair and brows, and upon his neck under the ear was a little raised pustule, from which a thin line of blood was streaked up to the angle of his cheek-bone.

Some instinctive feeling prompted Low to glance up at this moment. Half extended from the Museum doorway were a face and bony neck— a high-nosed, dull-eyed, malignant face, the eye-sockets hollow, and the darkened teeth showing. Low plunged his hand into his pocket, and a shot rang out in the echoing passage-way and hall. The wind sighed through the broken panes, a ribbon of stuff fluttered along the polished flooring, and that was all, as Flaxman Low half dragged, half carried Swaffam into the smoking-room.

It was some time before Swaffam recovered consciousness. He listened to Low's story of how he had found him with a red angry gleam in his sombre eyes.

"The ghost has scored off me," he said, with an odd, sullen laugh, "but now I fancy it's my turn! But before we adjourn to the Museum to examine the place, I will ask you to let me hear your notion of things. You have been right in

F

saying there was real danger. For myself I can only tell you that I felt something spring upon me, and I knew no more. Had this not happened I am afraid I should never have asked you a second time what your idea of the matter might be," he added with a sort of sulky frankness.

"There are two main indications," replied Low. "This strip of yellow bandage, which I have just now picked up from the passage floor, and the mark on your neck."

"What's that you say?" Swaffam rose quickly and examined his neck in a small glass beside the mantelshelf.

"Connect those two, and I think I can leave you to work it out for yourself," said Low.

"Pray let us have your theory in full," requested Swaffam shortly.

"Very well," answered Low good-humouredly—he thought Swaffam's annoyance natural in the circumstances—"The long, narrow figure which seemed to the Professor to be armless is developed on the next occasion. For Miss Van der Voort sees a bandaged arm and a dark hand with gleaming—which means, of course, gilded—nails. The clicking sound of the footsteps coincides with these particulars, for we know that sandals made of strips of leather are not uncommon in company with gilt nails and bandages. Old and dry leather would naturally click upon your polished floor."

"Bravo, Mr. Low! So you mean to say that this house is haunted by a mummy!"

"That is my idea, and all I have seen confirms me in my opinion."

"To do you justice, you held this theory before to-night—before, in fact, you had seen anything

for yourself.   You gathered that my father had
sent home a mummy, and you went on to conclude that I had opened the case ? "

"Yes.   I imagine you took off most of, or
rather all, the outer bandages, thus leaving the
limbs free, wrapped only in the inner bandages
which were swathed round each separate limb.
I fancy this mummy was preserved on the Theban
method with aromatic spices, which left the skin
olive-coloured, dry and flexible, like tanned
leather, the features remaining distinct, and the
hair, teeth, and eyebrows perfect."

"So far, good," said Swaffam.   "But now,
how about the intermittent vitality ?   The
pustule on the neck of those whom it attacks ?
And where is our old Baelbrow ghost to come
in ? "

Swaffam tried to speak in a rallying tone,
but his excitement and lowering temper were
visible enough, in spite of the attempts he made
to suppress them.

"To begin at the beginning," said Flaxman
Low, "everybody who, in a rational and honest
manner, investigates the phenomena of spiritism
will, sooner or later, meet in them some perplexing
element, which is not to be explained by any
of the ordinary theories.   For reasons into which
I need not now enter, this present case appears
to me to be one of these.   I am led to believe that
the ghost which has for so many years given
dim} and vague manifestations of its existence in
this house is a vampire."

Swaffam threw back his head with an
incredulous gesture.

"We no longer live in the middle ages, Mr,

Low ! And besides, how could a vampire come here ? " he said scoffingly.

" It is held by some authorities on these subjects that under certain conditions a vampire may be self-created. You tell me that this house is built upon an ancient barrow, in fact, on a spot where we might naturally expect to find such an elemental psychic germ. In those dead human systems were contained all the seeds for good and evil. The power which causes these psychic seeds or germs to grow is thought, and from being long dwelt on and indulged, a thought might finally gain a mysterious vitality, which could go on increasing more and more by attracting to itself suitable and appropriate elements from its environment. For a long period this germ remained a helpless intelligence, awaiting the opportunity to assume some material form, by means of which to carry out its desires. The invisible is the real ; the material only subserves its manifestation. The impalpable reality already existed, when you provided for it a physical medium for action by unwrapping the mummy's form. Now, we can only judge of the nature of the germ by its manifestation through matter. Here we have every indication of a vampire intelligence touching into life and energy the dead human frame. Hence the mark on the neck of its victims, and their bloodless and anæmic condition. For a vampire, as you know, sucks blood."

Swaffam rose, and took up the lamp.

" Now, for proof," he said bluntly. " Wait a second, Mr. Low. You say you fired at this appearance ? " And he took up the pistol which Low had laid down on the table.

" Yes, I aimed at a small portion of its foot which I saw on the step."

Without more words, and with the pistol still in his hand, Swaffam led the way to the Museum.

The wind howled round the house, and the darkness, which precedes the dawn, lay upon the world, when the two men looked upon one of the strangest sights it has ever been given to men to shudder at.

Half in and half out of an oblong wooden box in a corner of the great room, lay a lean shape in its rotten yellow bandages, the scraggy neck surmounted by a mop of frizzled hair. The toe strap of a sandal and a portion of the right foot had been shot away.

Swaffam, with a working face, gazed down at it, then seizing it by its tearing bandages, he flung it into the box, where it fell into a life-like posture, its wide, moist-lipped mouth gaping up at them.

For a moment Swaffam stood over the thing ; then with a curse he raised the revolver and shot into the grinning face again and again with a deliberate vindictiveness. Finally he rammed the thing down into the box, and, clubbing the weapon, smashed the head into fragments with a vicious energy that coloured the whole horrible scene with a suggestion of murder done.

Then, turning to Low, he said :

" Help me to fasten the cover on it."

" Are you going to bury it ? "

" No, we must rid the earth of it," he answered savagely. " I'll put it into the old canoe and burn it."

The rain had ceased when in the daybreak they carried the old canoe down to the shore.

In it they placed the mummy case with its ghastly
occupant, and piled faggots about it. The sail
was raised and the pile lighted, and Low and
Swaffam watched it creep out on the ebb-tide,
at first a twinkling spark, then a flare and waving
fire, until far out to sea the history of that dead
thing ended 3000 years after the priests of Armen
had laid it to rest in its appointed pyramid.

V

THE STORY OF THE GREY HOUSE

MR. FLAXMAN LOW declares that only on one occasion has he undertaken, unasked, the solving of a psychical mystery. To that case he always refers as the "affair of the Grey House." The house bears a different name in the annals of more than one scientific society, and much controversy has raged over the strange details of a story that seems to open up a new province of fantastic horror. Papers and treatises have been written about it in almost every European language, and many dismaying facts of a somewhat analogous nature have thus been brought to light. There was some hesitation at first about laying this matter—backed as it is by an explanation, which, though terrible, is not altogether unsupported—before the public, but it has finally been decided to incorporate it in the present book.

During the dry summer of 19—, Mr. Low happened to be staying in a lonely village on the coast of Devon. He was deeply immersed in some antiquarian work connected with the old Norse calendars, and therefore limited his acquaintance in the neighbourhood to one individual a Dr. Fremantle, who, besides being a medical man, was a botanist of some note.

One afternoon, when driving together, Mr. Low and Dr. Fremantle passed through a valley which nestled cup-like in the higher ground a few miles inland. As they passed along a deep, steep lane with overhanging hedges they caught a glimpse, through a break in the leaves, of a grey gable visible between the horizontal branches of a cedar.

Flaxman Low pointed it out to his companion.

"That's young Montesson's house," answered Fremantle, "and it bears a very sinister reputation. Nothing in your line, though," with a smile. "Indeed, no ghost would lend the same hideous associations to the place it now possesses as the result of a succession of mysterious murders that have occurred there."

"The grounds seem neglected. I don't remember to have seen such rank growth anywhere."

"Certainly not inside the British Isles," returned Fremantle. "The estate is left to take care of itself, partly because Montesson won't live there, partly because it is impossible to find labourers to work near the house. Our warm, damp climate and this sheltered position give rise to extraordinary luxuriance of growth. A stream runs along the bottom, and I expect all the low-lying land, where you see that belt of yellow African grass, is little better than a morass now."

Fremantle drew up as they gained the top of the slope. From there they could overlook the tangle of vegetation, dimmed by a rising mist, which surrounded and almost hid the roof of the Grey House.

" Yes," said Fremantle, in answer to an observation of Mr. Low, " Montesson's guardian, who lived here and looked after the property for him, turned the place into a subtropical garden. It used to be one of my chief pleasures to wander about here, but since my marriage my wife objects to my doing so, on account of the tales she has heard."

" What is the danger ? "

" Death ! " replied Fremantle shortly.

" What form of death ?   Malaria ? "

" No disease at all, my dear fellow. The persons who die at the Grey House are hanged by the neck until they are dead ! "

" Hanged ? " repeated Flaxman Low in surprise.

" Yes, hanged. Not only strangled but suspended, as the marks on the necks show.   If there were any hint of a ghost in it you might investigate—Montesson would be only too grateful if you could fathom the mystery."

" Tell me something more definite."

" I'll tell you what has happened within my own knowledge. Montesson's father died some fifteen years ago and left him to the guardianship of a cousin named Lampurt, who, as I told you, was a horticulturist, and planted the place with a wonderful variety of foreign shrubs and flowers. Lampurt had a bad name in the country, and his appearance was certainly against him—a squint-eyed, pig-faced fellow, who sidled along like a crab, and could not look you in the face. He died first."

" Was he hanged ?   Or did he hang himself ? "

" Neither, in this case. He dropped in a kind of fit, right up in front of the house, while he was engaged in planting some new acquisition.

Had it not been for the evidence of the persons
who were present at the time, I should have said
his death resulted from some tremendous mental
shock.   But the gardener and his relation,
Mrs. Montesson, agreed in saying that he was not
exerting himself unduly, and that he had had no
disturbing news. He was a healthy man and I
could see no sufficient reason for his death.
He was simply gardening, and had apparently
pricked himself with a nail for he had a spot
of blood upon his forefinger.

" After that all went well for a couple of years,
when, during the summer holidays the trouble
began.   Montesson must have been about sixteen
at the time, and had a tutor with him. His
mother and sister—a pretty girl rather older
than himself—were also here.   One morning
the girl was found lying on the gravel under her
window, quite dead. I was sent for, and, upon
examination, discovered the extraordinary fact
that she had been hanged ! "

" Murder ? "

" Of course, though we could find no trace
of the murderer. The girl had been taken from
her bedroom and hanged.   Then the rope was
removed and she was thrown in a heap under
her window. The crime caused a tremendous
sensation in the neighbourhood, and the police
were busy for a long time, but nothing came of
their inquiries.

" About a fortnight later, Platt, the tutor,
sat up smoking at the open study window.
In the morning he was found lying out over the
sill. There could be no mistake as to how he
met his death, for in addition to the deep line
round his throat, his neck was broken as neatly

as they could have done it at Newgate ! As
in the other case, there was nothing to show how
he came by his death, no rope, no trace of footsteps
or any struggle to lead one to suspect the presence
of another person or persons.   Yet from the facts
it could not have been suicide."

"I see you had some suspicion of your own,"
said Flaxman Low.

"Well, yes, I had.   But time has passed,
and I now think I must have been mistaken.
I must explain that the branches of the cedar
you saw jut to within a few feet of the windows
of the rooms occupied by Miss Montesson and
Platt respectively at the time of death.   I told
you there were no traces of anyone having
approached the house.   It therefore struck me
that some active person might have leaped from
the cedar into the open windows and escaped
in the same way, for the windows open vertically,
and when both leaves are thrown back, there is
a large aperture.   But the murders were so
purposeless and disconnected that they suggested
irresponsible agency.   I recollected Poë's story
of the Rue Morgue, where, you remember, the
crimes were committed by an ourang-outang.
It seemed to me possible that Lampurt, who was
of a morose and strange temper, might, among
other things, have secretly imported an ape and
turned it loose in the woods.   I had a thorough
search made in the park and grounds, but we
found nothing, and I have long ago abandoned
the theory."

Low thought silently over the story for some
time, then he asked for the dates of the three
deaths.   Fremantle answered categorically, and
it appeared that all had taken place about the

same season of the year—during summer, in fact. Upon this Mr. Low made an offer to investigate the affair on psychical lines, if Montesson made no objection. In answer to this message Montesson took the next train down to Devon, and begged to be allowed to accompany Mr. Low in his inquiries.

Flaxman Low quickly saw that Montesson might prove a very useful companion. He was a blonde, heavily-built man, and plainly possessed of a strong will and temper. Low put aside his books and went off at once with Montesson to have a closer look at the Grey House while the daylight lasted.

It is difficult to give any adequate impression of the teeming exuberance of wild and tangled growth through which they had to cut their way. Young, lush, sappy leafage overlay and half disguised the dank rottenness of the older vegetation beneath. After wading more than breast-high through the matted reeds, below which the spreading stream was fast reducing the land to a swamp, they emerged into a fairly open space that had once been the lawn round the house.

Here brambles and lusty weeds now grew abundantly under the untended trees. Curious shrubs and plants flourished here and there. As they came up a stoat sneaked away by a narrow footpath, nettle-grown and caked with damp, which led past blackened bushes round the house. Otherwise the place was deserted, not a leaf seemed to move in the windless heat of the afternoon. The squat, grey face of the house was scarred across by a dark-leaved creeper, hung with orchid-like blossoms, a little to the left of which Low noticed the cedar mentioned by Dr. Fremantle.

Low drew up at the weed-twisted, sunken little gate that gave upon the lawns and spoke for the first time.

"Tell me about it," and he nodded towards the house.

Montesson repeated the story already told, but added further details. "From here," went on Montesson, "you can see the exact spot where all these things took place. The upper of these two windows surrounded by the creeper and under the shadow of the cedar, belonged to my sister's room ; the lower is that of the study where Platt died. The gravel path below ran the whole length of the house, but it is now over-grown— Has Fremantle told you of Lawrence ? "

Low shook his head.

"I hate the very sight of the place ! " said Montesson hoarsely ; " the mystery and the horror of it all seem in my blood. I can't forget !— My mother left on the day of Platt's death, and has never been here since. But when I came of age I resolved to make another attempt to live here, meaning to sift the past if I got the chance of doing so. I had the grounds cleared about the house, and after leaving Oxford, came down with a man of my own year, called Lawrence. We spent the Easter vacation here reading, and all went right enough. Meanwhile I had the house examined, thinking there might be a secret entrance or room, but nothing of the kind exists. This house is not haunted. Nothing has ever been seen or heard of a supernatural character— nothing but the same awful repetition of blind murder ! "

After a few seconds he resumed.

"During the following summer Lawrence came down with me again. One hot evening we were smoking as we walked up and down the gravel under the windows. It was bright moonlight, and I remember the heavy scent of those red flowers—" Montesson glanced round him strangely.

"I went in to fetch a cigar. It took me some minutes to find the box I wanted, and to light the cigar. When I came out, Lawrence lay crumpled up as if he had fallen from a height, and he was dead. Round his neck was the same bluish line I had seen in the two other cases. You can understand what it was to leave the man not five minutes before, in health and strength, and to come back to find him dead—hanged—to judge from appearances! But as usual, no trace of rope or struggle or murderer!"

After some further talk, Mr. Low proposed to go into the house. It had evidently been deserted in haste. In the room once occupied by Miss Montesson, her girlish treasures still lay about, dusty, moth-eaten, and discoloured. Montesson paused on the threshold.

"Poor little Fan! It's just as she left it!" he said hurriedly.

The cedar outside threw a gloomy shade into the room, and the fantastic red blossoms drooped motionless in the stagnant air.

"Was the window open when your sister was found?" inquired Low after he had examined the room.

"Yes, it was hot weather—early in August. This room has not been occupied since. After Platt's affair, I have always avoided this side of the house, so that it was only by chance Lawrence and I came round to this part of the lawn to smoke."

" Then we may suppose that the danger, whatever it is, exists on this side of the house only ? "

" So it seems," replied Montesson.

" Your sister was last seen alive in this room ? Platt in the room directly below ? and your friend—what of him ? "

" Lawrence was lying on the gravel path just under the study window. All of them have died under the shadow of the cedar. Did Fremantle give you his idea ? Poor Lawrence's death disposed of that theory. No big ape could live in England all those five years in the open, and in any case it must have been seen sometime in the interval."

" I think so," replied Low, abstractedly. " Now as to what we must do to try and get at the meaning of all this. Do you feel equal, considering all you have gone through in this house, do you feel equal to remaining here with me for a night or two ? "

Montesson again glanced over his shoulder nervously.

" Yes," he said. " I know my nerves are not as stiff and steady as they should be, but I'll stand by you—especially as you would not find another man about here willing to run the risk. You see it is not a ghost or any fanciful trouble, it means a real danger. Think over it, Mr. Low, before you undertake so hazardous an attempt."

Low looked into the blue eyes Montesson had fixed upon him. They were weary, anxious eyes, and, taken in combination with his compressed

lips and square chin, told Low of the struggle
this man constantly endured between his shaken
nervous system and the strong will that mastered
it.

"If you'll stand by me, I'll try to get, to the
bottom of it," said Low.

"I wonder if I should allow you to risk your
life in this way?" returned Montesson, passing
his hand over his prematurely-lined forehead.

"Why not? Besides it is my own wish. As
for risking our lives—it is for the good of man-
kind."

"I can't say I see it in that light," said
Montesson in surprise.

"If we lose our lives it will be in the effort
to make another spot of earth clean and wholesome and safe for men to live on. Our duty
to the public requires us to run a murderer to
earth. Here we have a murderous power of
some subtle kind; it is not quite as much our
duty to destroy it if we can, even at risk to
ourselves?"

The result of this conversation was an arrangement to pass the night at the Grey House. About
ten o'clock they set out, intending to follow the
path they had more or less successfully cleared
for themselves in the afternoon. By Flaxman
Low's advice, Montesson carried a long knife.
The night was unusually hot and still, and lit
only by a thin moon as they made their way along,
stumbling over matted weeds and roots and literally feeling for the path, until they came to the
little gate by the lawn. There they stopped a
moment to look at the house, standing out among
its strange sea of overgrowth, the dim moon
low on the horizon, glinting palely upon the

windows and over the deserted countryside. As they waited a night-bird hooted and flapped its way across the open.

At any moment they might be at hand-grips with the mysterious power of death which haunted the place. The warm lush-scented air and the sinister shadows seemed charged with some ominous influence. As they drew near the house Low perceived a sweet, heavy odour.

"What is it ? " he asked.

"It comes from those scarlet flowers, at night. It's unbearable !   Lampurt imported the thing," replied Montesson irritably.

"Which room will you spend the night in ? " asked Low as they gained the hall.

Montesson hesitated. "Have you ever heard the expression ' grey with fear ' ? " he said, laughing in the dark ; " I'm that ! "

Low did not like the laugh, it was only one remove, and that a very little one, from hysteria.

"We won't find out much unless we each remain alone, and with open windows as they did," said Low.

Montesson shook himself.

"No, I suppose not. *They* were each alone when—good-night, I'll call if anything happens, and you must do the same for me. For Heaven's sake, don't go to sleep ! "

"And remember," added Low, "with your knife to cut at anything that touches you." Then he stood at the study door and listened to Montesson's heavy steps as they passed up the stairs, for he had elected to pass the night in his sister's room. Low heard him walk across the floor above and throw wide the window.

When Mr. Low turned into the study and

G

tried to open the window there, he found it impossible to do so, the creeper outside had fastened upon the woodwork, binding the sashes together. There was but one thing left for him to do, he must go outside and stand where Lawrence had stood on the fatal night. He let himself out softly and went round to the south side of the house.

There he paced up and down in the shadows for perhaps an hour.

In the deceptive, iridescent moonlight a pallid head seemed to wag at him from the gloom below the cedar, but, moving towards it, he grasped only the yellow bunched blossom of a giant ragwort. Then he stood still and looked up into the branches above; the gnarled black branches with their fringes of black sticky leaves. Fremantle's theory of the ape passing stealthily among them to spring upon his victims found a sudden horror of possibility in Low's mind. He imagined the girl awaking in the brute's cruel hands——

Out upon the quiet brooding of the night broke a scream—or rather a roar, a harsh, jagged, pulsating roar, that ceased as abruptly as it had begun.

Without a moment's consideration, Mr. Low seized the branch nearest to him and, swinging himself up into the tree, he climbed with a frantic effort towards the window of Montesson's room, from which he was almost sure the sound had come. Being an unusually active and athletic man he leaped from the branch towards the open window, and fell headlong in upon the floor. As he did so, something seemed to pass him, something swift and sinuous that might have been a snake, and disappear out of the window !

Remembering a candle on the toilet table, he lit it when he regained his feet and looked about him.

Montesson lay on the floor " crumpled up," as he had himself described Lawrence's position. Low recalled this with misgiving as he hurried to his side. A dark smear like blood was on Montesson's cheek, but though unconscious, he was still alive. Low lifted him on to the bed and did what he could to rouse him, but without success. He lay rigid, breathing the slow almost imperceptible respiration of deep stupor.

Low was about to go to the window, when the candle suddenly went out, and he was left in the increasing darkness, to all intents alone, to face an unknown though tangible assailant.

Silence had again fallen upon the house—that is, the silence of night, and woodlands, and many-folded leafage, and the things that go by night. He stood by the window and listened. His senses were acute and throbbing ; he felt as if he could hear for miles. The scent of the scarlet blossoms rose like deadening fumes into his brain, and he drew away from the window, and, feeling strangely spent, threw himself upon a couch. Then he drew out the knife at his belt, and strung himself up to watchfulness with an effort.

He knew that the attack he had to expect would be likely to come from the direction of the window. He saw the faint, swimming moon-light that fell through the leaves and tendrils of the creeper fade slowly away. Probably clouds

were coming up over the sky, for the steamy
heat was even more oppressive.

The low window-sill was scarcely more than
a foot above the floor, and presently he fancied
something was moving along the carpet among
the entangling shadows of the leaves, but the
darkness was now intensified, and he could
not be sure. Montesson's breathing had become
quieter. It was the dead hour of the night;
hardly a sound was to be heard.

Suddenly Low felt a soft touch upon his knee.
His whole consciousness had been so absorbed
in the act of listening that this unexpected
appeal to another sense startled him. Here
and there, rapid, soft, and light, the touches
passed over his body. It might have been
some animal nosing about him in the dark. Then
a smooth, cold touch fell upon his cheek.

Low sprang up, and slashed about him in the
darkness with his knife.

In that instant the thing closed with him—a
flexuous, snaky thing that flung its coils about
his limbs and body in one swift spring like a
curling whiplash !

Flaxman Low was all but helpless in the
winding grasp of what ?—the tentacles of
some strange creature ? or was it some great
snake, this sentient thing that was feeling for
his throat ? There was not an instant to lose.
The knife was pressed against his body; with a
violent effort he drew it sharply, edge outwards,
against the tightening coils. A spurt of clammy
fluid fell upon his hand, and the thing loosed
and fell away from him into the stifling gloom.

In the morning Montesson came to himself in

one of the lower rooms at the other side of the house. Fremantle was beside him.

"What's the matter?" he asked. "Ah, I remember now. There's Low. It has beaten us again, Fremantle! It is hopeless. I don't know what happened—I was not asleep, when I found myself seized, lifted up, drawn towards the window, and strangled by loving ropes. Look at Low!" he went on harshly, raising himself. "Why, man, you're all over blood!"

Flaxman Low glanced down at his hands.

"Looks like it," he said.

"It has beaten even you, Low!" went on Montesson. "There is something much more terrible and tangible than a ghost in this cursed house! See here!"

He pulled down his collar. A faint bluish circle with suffused dots was drawn round his throat.

"It is some deadly species of snake," exclaimed Fremantle.

Low sat down astride a chair thoughtfully.

"I'm sorry to disagree with both of you. But I am inclined to think it is not a snake, and on the other hand I fancy it has a great deal to do with what we may roughly call a ghost. The whole evidence points in only one direction."

"You mustn't let your prejudice in favour of physical problems run away with your reason," said Fremantle drily. "Has a ghost actual, palpable power?—to go further, has it blood?"

Montesson, who had been looking at his neck in the glass, turned quickly. "It's some horrible thing in nature! Something between a snake and an octopus ! What do you say to it, Low ? "

Low looked up gravely.

" In spite of Fremantle's objections the steps from beginning to end are very clear."

Fremantle and Montesson exchanged a glance of incredulity.

" My dear fellow, much learning has warped your mind," said Fremantle with an embarrassed laugh.

" First of all," continued Low," we know where all the deaths have occurred."

" To speak precisely, they have all occurred in different places," interposed Fremantle.

" True ; but within a strictly limited area. The slight differences have been of material help to me. In all cases they have occurred in the vicinity of one thing."

" The cedar ! " cried Montesson, with some excitement.

" That was my first idea—now I refer to the wall. Will you tell me the probable weight of Lawrence and Platt at the date of death ? "

" Platt was a small man—perhaps under nine stone. Lawrence, though much taller, was thin, and could not have weighed more than eleven. As for poor little Fan, she was only a slip of a girl."

" Three people have been killed—one has escaped. In what way do you differ from the others, Montesson ? " asked Low.

" If you mean I'm heavier, I certainly am. I scale something like fifteen. But what has that to do with it ? "

" Everything. The coils have evidently not sufficient compressive power to destroy life by strangulation simply—there must be suspension as well. You were simply too heavy for them to tackle."

" Coils of what ? "

" Of this." Low held up a tapering, reddish-brown tendon or line, which had red curved triangular teeth set on it at intervals.

The two other men stared at this object, and then Montesson burst out : " The creeper on the wall ! " he said, in a tone of disappointment. " It couldn't be ! Besides, has a plant blood ? "

" Let us go and look at it," said Low. " This creeper has never been cut because it withers away every winter to the ground and grows again in the spring. Look here ! " He took out his knife and cut a leathery shoot. A crimson stain spurted out on his cuff. " The only person, as far as I can gather, who cut this plant was Mr. Lampurt in nailing it to the wall. He died of shock when he saw the red stain on his finger, as he knew something of its deadly properties. But though stupefying—as your condition last night proved, Montesson—they are not fatal. Even to stupefy they must get into the blood. Now the deaths have all occurred within reach of the tendrils of this plant. And all have happened at the same season of the year, that is to say, at the time when it attains its full annual strength and growth. Another point in favour of Montesson's escape was the dryness of the season. The growth is not quite so good as usual this summer, is it ? "

" No, the tendrils are thinner—a good deal thinner and smaller."

" Just so. Therefore your weight saved you, though you were stupefied by the punctures of the thorns. I feared that, and warned you to use your knife."

"But the brain of the thing ? " cried Fremantle. "Why, man, has a plant will and knowledge and malevolence ? "

"Not of itself, as I believe," answered Low. "Perhaps you will prefer to attribute much to the long arm of coincidence, but the explanation I can offer is one that has long been held by occultists in other countries. Pythagoras and others have taught that the forms of incarnation change as the soul raises or debases itself during each spell of Life. Connect with this the belief of the Brahmins, and I may add of various African tribes, that an earth-bound spirit, at the moment of a premature or sudden death, may pass into plants or trees of certain species, by virtue of an inherent attraction possessed by these plants for such entities. To go further, it is said that these degraded souls have intervals during which they have power of voluntary action to do good or evil, and such action has influence on their future incarnations."

"What do you mean ? What do you intend us to believe ? " Montesson said, and stopped.

"It is hard to put it into words in these latter days of unbelief," said Low, "but the evidence goes to show that a man—presumably not a good man—dies a sudden death near this plant, even inoculated with its sap. Fremantle knows this plant to be a Malayan creeper, belonging to a family that possess strange power and properties. I may recall the old story of the upas tree, and more lately still the murder tree discovered near Kolwe, in East Africa, by Herr Boltze. There are also other instances."

" It is incredible ! " said Fremantle almost angrily.

" I don't ask you to believe it," said Flaxman Low quietly, " I only tell you such beliefs exist. Montesson can do something towards proving my theory. Let him have the plant destroyed, and judge by the results."

The tendril of the creeper severed by Mr. Low in his struggle was presented by him to the authorities at Kew.

Mr. Montesson has acted upon Mr. Flaxman Low's suggestions. The Grey House is now occupied and safe, and it is a strange fact that no plant, not even the hardy ivy, will live where the red-blossomed creeper once grew.

VI

THE STORY OF YAND MANOR
HOUSE

LOOKING through the notes of Mr. Flaxman
Low, one sometimes catches through the steel-
blue hardness of facts, the pink flush of romance,
or more often the black corner of a horror un-
nameable. The following story may serve as
an instance of the latter. Mr. Low not only
unravelled the mystery at Yand, but at the same
time justified his life-work to M. Thierry, the
well-known French critic and philosopher.

At the end of a long conversation, M. Thierry,
arguing from his own standpoint as a materialist,
had said :

"The factor in the human economy which
you call ' soul ' cannot be placed."

"I admit that," replied Low. "Yet, when
a man dies, is there not one factor unaccounted
for in the change that comes upon him ? Yes !
For though his body still exists, it rapidly falls
to pieces, which proves that that has gone which
held it together."

The Frenchman laughed, and shifted his
ground.

"Well, for my part, I don't believe in ghosts !

Spirit manifestations, occult phenomena—is not
this the ashbin into which a certain clique shoot
everything they cannot understand, or for which
they fail to account ? "

"Then what should you say to me, Monsieur,
if I told you that I have passed a good portion
of my life in investigating this particular ashbin,
and have been lucky enough to sort a small part
of its contents with tolerable success ? " replied
Flaxman Low.

"The subject is doubtless interesting—but I
should like to have some personal experience
in the matter," said Thierry dubiously.

"I am at present investigating a most singular
case," said Low. "Have you a day or two to
spare ? "

Thierry thought for a minute or more.

"I am grateful," he replied. "But, forgive
me, is it a convincing ghost ? "

"Come with me to Yand and see. I have
been there once already, and came away for the
purpose of procuring information from MSS.
to which I have the privilege of access, for I
confess that the phenomena at Yand lie altogether outside any former experience of mine."

Low sank back into his chair with his hands
clasped behind his head—a favourite position
of his—and the smoke of his long pipe curled
up lazily into the golden face of an Isis, which
stood behind him on a bracket. Thierry, glancing
across, was struck by the strange likeness between
the faces of the Egyptian goddess and this scientist
of the nineteenth century. On both rested the
calm, mysterious abstraction of some unfathomable
thought. As he looked, he decided.

"I have three days to place at your disposal."

"I thank you heartily," replied Low. "To be associated with so brilliant a logician as yourself in an inquiry of this nature is more than I could have hoped for! The material with which I have to deal is so elusive, the whole subject is wrapped in such obscurity and hampered by so much prejudice, that I can find few really qualified persons who care to approach these investigations seriously. I go down to Yand this evening, and hope not to leave without clearing up the mystery. You will accompany me?"

"Most certainly. Meanwhile pray tell me something of the affair."

"Briefly the story is as follows. Some weeks ago I went to Yand Manor House at the request of the owner, Sir George Blackburton, to see what I could make of the events which took place there. All they complain of is the impossibility of remaining in one room,—the dining-room."

"What then is he like, this M. le Spook?" asked the Frenchman, laughing.

"No one has ever seen him, or for that matter heard him."

"Then how——"

"You can't see him, nor hear him, nor smell him," went on Low, "but you can feel him and —taste him!"

"*Mon Dieu!* But this is singular! Is he then of so bad a flavour?"

"You shall taste for yourself," answered Flaxman Low smiling. "After a certain hour no one can remain in the room, they are simply crowded out."

"But who crowds them out?" asked Thierry.

"That is just what I hope we may discover to-night or to-morrrow."

The last train that night dropped Mr. Flaxman Low and his companion at a little station near Yand. It was late, but a trap in waiting soon carried them to the Manor House. The big bulk of the building stood up in absolute blackness before them.

"Blackburton was to have met us, but I suppose he has not yet arrived," said Low. "Hullo! the door is open," he added as he stepped into the hall.

Beyond a dividing curtain they now perceived a light. Passing behind this curtain they found themselves at the end of the long hall, the wide staircase opening up in front of them.

"But who is this?" exclaimed Thierry.

Swaying and stumbling at every step, there tottered slowly down the stairs the figure of a man. He looked as if he had been drinking, his face was livid, and his eyes sunk into his head.

"Thank Heaven you've come! I heard you outside," he said in a weak voice.

"It's Sir George Blackburton," said Low, as the man lurched forward and pitched into his arms.

They laid him down on the rugs and tried to restore consciousness.

"He has the air of being drunk, but it is not so," remarked Thierry. "Monsieur has had a bad shock of the nerves. See the pulses drumming in his throat."

In a few minutes Blackburton opened his eyes and staggered to his feet.

"Come. I could not remain there alone. Come quickly."

They went rapidly across the hall, Blackburton leading the way down a wide passage to a double-leaved door, which, after a perceptible pause, he threw open, and they all entered together.

On the great table in the centre stood an extinguished lamp, some scattered food, and a big, lighted candle. But the eyes of all three men passed at once to a dark recess beside the heavy, carved chimneypiece, where a rigid shape sat perched on the back of a huge, oak chair.

Flaxman Low snatched up the candle and crossed the room towards it.

On the top of the chair, with his feet upon the arms, sat a powerfully-built young man huddled up. His mouth was open, and his eyes twisted upwards. Nothing further could be seen from below but the ghastly pallor of cheek and throat.

"Who is this?" cried Low. Then he laid his hand gently on the man's knee.

At the touch the figure collapsed in a heap upon the floor, the gaping, set, terrified face turned up to theirs.

"He's dead!" said Low after a hasty examination. "I should say he's been dead some hours."

"Oh, Lord! Poor Batty!" groaned Sir George, who was entirely unnerved. "I'm glad you've come."

"Who is he?" said Thierry, "and what was he doing here?"

"He's a gamekeeper of mine. He was always anxious to try conclusions with the ghost, and last night he begged me to lock him in here with food for twenty-four hours. I refused at first, but then I thought if anything happened while he was in here alone, it would interest you. Who could imagine it would end like this ? ''

" When did you find him ? '' asked Low.

" I only got here from my mother's half an hour ago. I turned on the light in the hall and came in here with a candle. As I entered the room, the candle went out, and—and—I think I must be going mad."

" Tell us everything you saw," urged Low.

" You will think I am beside myself ; but as the light went out and I sank almost paralysed into an armchair, I saw two barred eyes looking at me ! ''

" Barred eyes ? What do you mean ? ''

" Eyes that looked at me through thin vertical bars, like the bars of a cage. What's that ? ''

With a smothered yell Sir George sprang back. He had approached the dead man and declared something had brushed his face.

" You were standing on this spot under the overmantel. I will remain here. Meantime, my dear Thierry, I feel sure you will help Sir George to carry this poor fellow to some more suitable place," said Flaxman Low.

When the dead body of the young gamekeeper had been carried out, Low passed slowly round and about the room. At length he stood under the old carved overmantel, which reached to the ceiling and projected bodily forward in quaint heads of satyrs and animals. One of these on the side nearest the recess represented a griffin with a flanged mouth. Sir George had been standing directly below this at the moment

when he felt the touch on his face. Now alone
in the dim, wide room, Flaxman Low stood on
the same spot and waited. The candle threw
its dull yellow rays on the shadows which seemed
to gather closer and wait also. Presently a
distant door banged, and Low, leaning forward
to listen, distinctly felt something on the back of
his neck !

He swung round. There was nothing ! He
searched carefully on all sides, then put his
hand up to the griffin's head. Again came the
same soft touch, this time upon his hand, as if
something had floated past on the air.

This was definite. The griffin's head located
it. Taking the candle to examine more closely,
Low found four long black hairs depending from
the jagged fangs. He was detaching them when
Thierry reappeared.

"We must get Sir George away as soon as
possible," he said.

"Yes, we must take him away, I fear," agreed
Low. "Our investigation must be put off till
to-morrow."

On the following day they returned to Yand.
It was a large country-house, pretty and old-
fashioned, with lattice windows and deep gables,
that looked out between tall shrubs and across
lawns set with beaupots, where peacocks sunned
themselves on the velvet turf. The church
spire peered over the trees on one side ; and an
old wall covered with ivy and creeping plants,
and pierced at intervals with arches, alone separated
the gardens from the churchyard.

The haunted room lay at the back of the house.
It was square and handsome, and furnished in
the style of the last century. The oak overmantel

reached to the ceiling, and a wide window, which almost filled one side of the room, gave a view of the west door of the church.

Low stood for a moment at the open window looking out at the level sunlight which flooded the lawns and parterres.

" See that door sunk in the church wall to the left ? " said Sir George's voice at his elbow. " That is the door of the family vault. Cheerful outlook, isn't it ? "

" I should like to walk across there presently," remarked Low.

" What ! Into the vault ? " asked Sir George, with a harsh laugh. " I'll take you if you like. Anything else I can show you or tell you ? "

" Yes. Last night I found this hanging from the griffin's head," said Low, producing the thin wisp of black hair. " It must have touched your cheek as you stood below. Do you know to whom it can belong ? "

" It's a woman's hair ! No, the only woman who has been in this room to my knowledge for months is an old servant with grey hair, who cleans it," returned Blackburton. " I'm sure it was not here when I locked Batty in."

" It is human hair, exceedingly coarse and long uncut," said Low ; " but it is not necessarily a woman's."

" It is not mine at any rate, for I'm sandy ; and poor Batty was fair. Good-night ; I'll come round for you in the morning."

Presently, when the night closed in, Thierry and Low settled down in the haunted room to await developments. They smoked and talked deep into the night. A big lamp burned brightly

H

on the table, and the surroundings looked homely
and desirable.

Thierry made a remark to that effect, adding
that perhaps the ghost might see fit to omit
his usual visit.

" Experience goes to prove that ghosts have
a cunning habit of choosing persons either
credulous or excitable to experiment upon," he
added.

To M. Thierry's surprise, Flaxman Low agreed
with him.

" They certainly choose suitable persons," he
said, " that is, not credulous persons, but those
whose senses are sufficiently keen to detect the
presence of a spirit. In my own investigations,
I try to eliminate what you would call the supernatural element. I deal with these mysterious
affairs as far as possible on material lines."

" Then what do you say of Batty's death ?
He died of fright—simply."

" I hardly think so. The manner of his death
agrees in a peculiar manner with what we know
of the terrible history of this room. He died
of fright and pressure combined. Did you hear
the doctor's remark ? It was significant. He
said : ' The indications are precisely those I
have observed in persons who have been crushed
and killed in a crowd ! ' "

" That is sufficiently curious, I allow. I see
that it is already past two o'clock. I am thirsty ;
I will have a little seltzer." Thierry rose from
his chair, and, going to the side-board, drew
a tumblerful from the syphon. " Pah ! What
an abominable taste ! "

" What ? The seltzer ? "

" Not at all ? " returned the Frenchman

irritably. "I have not touched it yet. Some
horrible fly has flown into my mouth, I suppose.
Pah! Disgusting!"

"What is it like?" asked Flaxman Low, who
was at the moment wiping his own mouth with
his handkerchief.

"Like? As if some repulsive fungus had
burst in the mouth."

"Exactly. I perceive it also. I hope you
are about to be convinced."

"What?" exclaimed Thierry, turning his
big figure round and staring at Low. "You
don't mean——"

As he spoke the lamp suddenly went out.

"Why, then, have you put the lamp out at
such a moment?" cried Thierry.

"I have not put it out. Light the candle
beside you on the table."

Low heard the Frenchman's grunt of satisfaction as he found the candle, then the scratch
of a match. It sputtered and went out. Another
match and another behaved in the same manner,
while Thierry swore freely under his breath.

"Let me have your matches, Monsieur
Flaxman; mine are, no doubt, damp," he said
at last.

Low rose to feel his way across the room.
The darkness was dense.

"It is the darkness of Egypt,—it may be felt.
Where then are you, my dear friend?" he heard
Thierry saying, but the voice seemed a long way
off.

"I am coming," he answered, "but it's so
hard to get along."

After Low had spoken the words, their meaning
struck him. He paused and tried to realise in

what part of the room he was. The silence was
profound, and the growing sense of oppression
seemed like a nightmare. Thierry's voice sounded
again, faint and receding.

"I am suffocating, Monsieur Flaxman, where
are you ? I am near the door. Ach ! "

A strangling bellow of pain and fear followed,
that scarcely reached Low through the thickening
atmosphere.

"Thierry, what is the matter with you ? "
he shouted. "Open the door."

But there was no answer. What had become
of Thierry in that hideous, clogging gloom !
Was he also dead, crushed in some ghastly
fashion against the wall ? What was this ?

The air had become palpable to the touch,
heavy, repulsive, with the sensation of cold,
humid flesh !

Low pushed out his hands with a mad longing
to touch a table, a chair, anything but this clammy,
swelling softness that thrust itself upon him from
every side, baffling him and filling his grasp.

He knew now that he was absolutely alone
—struggling against what ?

His feet were slipping in his wild efforts to feel
the floor—the dank flesh was creeping upon his
neck, his cheek—his breath came short and labour-
ing as the pressure swung him gently to and fro,
helpless, nauseated !

The clammy flesh crowded upon him like the
bulk of some fat, horrible creature ; then came a
stinging pain on the cheek. Low clutched at
something—there was a crash and a rush of
air——

The next sensation of which Mr. Flaxman Low
was conscious was one of deathly sickness. He

was lying on wet grass, the wind blowing over
him, and all the clean, wholesome smells of the
open air in his nostrils.

He sat up and looked about him. Dawn was
breaking windily in the east, and by its light he
saw that he was on the lawn of Yand Manor
House. The latticed window of the haunted
room above him was open. He tried to remember
what had happened. He took stock of himself,
in fact, and slowly felt that he still held something
clutched in his right hand—something dark-
coloured, slender, and twisted. It might have
been a long shred of bark or the cast skin of an
adder—it was impossible to see in the dim light.

After an interval the recollection of Thierry
recurred to him. Scrambling to his feet, he
raised himself to the window sill and looked in.
Contrary to his expectation, there was no upset-
ting of furniture ; everything remained in position
as when the lamp went out. His own chair
and the one Thierry had occupied were just as
when they had arisen from them. But there
was no sign of Thierry.

Low jumped in by the window. There was
the tumbler full of seltzer, and the litter of matches
about it. He took up Thierry's box of matches
and struck a light. It flared, and he lit the candle
with ease. In fact, everything about the room
was perfectly normal ; all the horrible conditions
prevailing but a couple of hours ago had
disappeared.

But where was Thierry ? Carrying the lighted
candle, he passed out of the door, and searched
in the adjoining rooms. In one of them, to his
relief, he found the Frenchman sleeping pro-
foundly in an armchair.

Low touched his arm. Thierry leapt to his feet, fending off an imaginary blow with his arm. Then he turned his scared face on Low.

"What! You, Monsieur Flaxman! How have you escaped?"

"I should rather ask you how you escaped," said Low, smiling at the havoc the night's experiences had worked in his friend's looks and spirits.

"I was crowded out of the room against the door. That infernal thing—what was it?—with its damp, swelling flesh, inclosed me!" A shudder of disgust stopped him. "I was a fly in an aspic. I could not move. I sank into the stifling pulp. The air grew thick. I called to you, but your answers became inaudible. Then I was suddenly thrust against the door by a huge hand—it felt like one, at least. I had a struggle for my life, I was all but crushed, and then, I do not know how, I found myself outside the door. I shouted to you in vain. Therefore, as I could not help you, I came here, and—I will confess it, my dear friend—I locked and bolted the door. After some time I went again into the hall and listened ; but, as I heard nothing, I resolved to wait until daylight and the return of Sir George."

"That's all right," said Low. "It was an experience worth having."

"But, no! Not for me! I do not envy you your researches into mysteries of this abominable description. I now comprehend perfectly that Sir George has lost his nerve if he has had to do with this horror. Besides, it is entirely impossible to explain these things."

At this moment they heard Sir George's arrival, and went out to meet him.

"I could not sleep all night for thinking of you!" exclaimed Blackburton on seeing them; "and I came along as soon as it was light. Something has happened."

"But certainly something has happened," cried M. Thierry shaking his head solemnly; "something of the most bizarre, of the most horrible! Monsieur Flaxman, you shall tell Sir George this story. You have been in that accursed room all night, and remain alive to tell the tale!"

As Low came to the conclusion of the story Sir George suddenly exclaimed:

"You have met with some injury to your face, Mr. Low."

Low turned to the mirror. In the now strong light three parallel weals from eye to mouth could be seen.

"I remember a stinging pain like a lash on my cheek. What would you say these marks were caused by, Thierry?" asked Low.

Thierry looked at them and shook his head.

"No one in their senses would venture to offer any explanation of the occurrences of last night," he replied.

"Something of this sort, do you think?" asked Low again, putting down the object he held in his hand on the table.

Thierry took it up and described it aloud.

"A long and thin object of a brown and yellow colour and twisted like a sabre-bladed corkscrew," then he started slightly and glanced at Low.

"It's a human nail, I imagine," suggested Low.

"But no human being has talons of this kind —except, perhaps, a Chinaman of high rank."

"There are no Chinamen about here, nor ever have been, to my knowledge," said Blackburton shortly, "I'm very much afraid that, in spite of all you have so bravely faced, we are no nearer to any rational explanation."

"On the contrary, I fancy I begin to see my way. I believe, after all, that I may be able to convert you, Thierry," said Flaxman Low.

"Convert me ?"

"To a belief in the definite aim of my work. But you shall judge for yourself. What do you make of it so far ? I claim that you know as much of the matter as I do."

"My dear good friend, I make nothing of it," returned Thierry, shrugging his shoulders and spreading out his hands. "Here we have a tissue of unprecedented incidents that can be explained on no theory whatever."

"But this is definite," and Flaxman Low held up the blackened nail.

"And how do you propose to connect that nail with the black hairs—with the eyes that looked through the bars of a cage—the fate of Batty, with its symptoms of death by pressure and suffocation—our experience of swelling flesh, that something which filled and filled the room to the exclusion of all else ? How are you going to account for these things by any kind of connected hypothesis ?" asked Thierry, with a shade of irony.

"I mean to try," replied Low.

At lunch time Thierry inquired how the theory was getting on.

"It progresses," answered Low. "By the way, Sir George, who lived in this house for some time prior to, say, 1840 ? He was a man—it

may have been a woman, but, from the nature of
his studies, I am inclined to think it was a man—
who was deeply read in ancient necromancy,
eastern magic, mesmerism, and subjects of a
kindred nature. And was he not buried in the
vault you pointed out ? "

" Do you know anything more about him ? "
asked Sir George in surprise.

" He was I imagine," went on Flaxman Low
reflectively, " hirsute and swarthy, probably a
recluse, and suffered from a morbid and extrava-
gant fear of death."

" How do you know all this ? "

" I only asked about it. Am I right ? "

" You have described my cousin, Sir Gilbert
Blackburton, in every particular. I can show
you his portrait in another room."

As they stood looking at the painting of Sir
Gilbert Blackburton, with his long, melancholy,
olive face and thick, black beard, Sir George
went on. " My grandfather succeeded him at
Yand. I have often heard my father speak of
Sir Gilbert, and his strange studies and extraordinary fear of death. Oddly enough, in the end
he died rather suddenly, while he was still hale
and strong. He predicted his own approaching
death, and had a doctor in attendance for a
week or two before he died. He was placed in
a coffin he had had made on some plan of his own
and buried in the vault. His death occurred in
1842 or 1843. If you care to see them I can shew
you some of his papers, which may interest
you."

Mr. Flaxman Low spent the afternoon over the
papers. When evening came, he rose from his
work with a sigh of content, stretched himself,

and joined Thierry and Sir George in the garden.

They dined at Lady Blackburton's, and it was late before Sir George found himself alone with Mr. Flaxman Low and his friend.

"Have you formed any opinion about the thing which haunts the Manor House?" he asked anxiously.

Thierry elaborated a cigarette, crossed his legs, and added :

"If you have in truth come to any definite conclusion, pray let us hear it, my dear Monsieur Flaxman."

"I have reached a very definite and satisfactory conclusion," replied Low. "The Manor House is haunted by Sir Gilbert Blackburton, who died, or, rather, who seemed to die, on the 15th of August, 1842."

"Nonsense! The nail fifteen inches long at the least—how do you connect it with Sir Gilbert?" asked Blackburton testily.

"I am convinced that it belonged to Sir Gilbert," Low answered.

"But the long black hair like a woman's?"

"Dissolution in the case of Sir Gilbert was not complete—not consummated, so to speak —as I hope to show you later. Even in the case of dead persons the hair and nails have been known to grow. By a rough calculation as to the growth of nails in such cases, I was enabled to indicate approximately the date of Sir Gilbert's death. The hair too grow on his head."

"But the barred eyes? I saw them myself!" exclaimed the young man.

"The eyelashes grow also. You follow me?"

"You have, I presume, some theory in connection with this ? " observed Thierry. "It must be a very curious one."

" Sir Gilbert in his fear of death appears to have mastered and elaborated a strange and ancient formula by which the grosser factors of the body being eliminated, the more ethereal portions continue to retain the spirit, and the body is thus preserved from absolute disintegration. In this manner true death may be indefinitely deferred. Secure from the ordinary chances and changes of existence, this spiritualised body could retain a modified life practically for ever."

" This is a most extraordinary idea, my dear fellow," remarked Thierry.

" But why should Sir Gilbert haunt the Manor House, and one special room ? "

" The tendency of spirits to return to the old haunts of bodily life is almost universal. We cannot yet explain the reason of this attraction of environment."

" But the expansion—the crowding substance which we ourselves felt ? You cannot meet that difficulty," said Thierry persistently.

" Not as fully as I could wish, perhaps. But the power of expanding and contracting to a degree far beyond our comprehension is a well-known attribute of spiritualised matter."

" Wait one little moment, my dear Monsieur Flaxman," broke in Thierry's voice after an interval ; " this is very clever and ingenious indeed. As a theory I give it my sincere admiration. But proof—proof is what we now demand."

Flaxman Low looked steadily at the two incredulous faces.

"This," he said slowly, "is the hair of Sir Gilbert Blackburton, and this nail is from the little finger of his left hand. You can prove my assertion by opening the coffin."

Sir George, who was pacing up and down the room impatiently, drew up.

"I don't like it at all, Mr. Low, I tell you frankly. I don't like it at all. I see no object in violating the coffin. I am not concerned to verify this unpleasant theory of yours. I have only one desire ; I want to get rid of this haunting presence, whatever it is."

"If I am right," replied Low, "the opening of the coffin and exposure of the remains to strong sunshine for a short time will free you for ever from this presence."

In the early morning, when the summer sun struck warmly on the lawns of Yand, the three men carried the coffin from the vault to a quiet spot among the shrubs where, secure from observation, they raised the lid.

Within the coffin lay the semblance of Gilbert Blackburton, maned to the ears with long and coarse black hair. Mattered eyelashes swept the fallen cheeks, and beside the body stretched the bony hands, each with its dependent sheaf of switch-like nails. Low bent over and raised the left hand gingerly.

The little finger was without a nail !

Two hours later they came back and looked again. The sun had in the meantime done its work ; nothing remained but a fleshless skeleton and a few half-rotten shreds of clothing.

The ghost of Yand Manor House has never since been heard of.

When Thierry bade Flaxman Low good-bye, he said :

" In time, my dear Monsieur Flaxman, you will add another to our sciences. You establish your facts too well for my peace of mind."

MILLER, SON, AND COMPY., LIMITED,
PRINTERS,
FAKENHAM AND LONDON.

www.ingramcontent.com/pod-product-compliance
Lightning Source LLC
Chambersburg PA
CBHW020149180626
46810CB00004B/1803